THE DARK
OFFICE

By the same author

Like time-travel?

Check out the Turning Points series
at jodielane.com

The Siege of Masada
Transylvanian Knight
To Kill An Emperor
Renaissance Woman
Heart and Stomach of a Queen

THE DARK OFFICE

AND OTHER TALES

JODIE LANE

CONTENTS

THE DARK OFFICE

Crick Sema paused at the bottom of the basement steps and flipped the switch. He waited as the ancient fluoro flickered and hummed to life, bringing the reception area into view. Crick (short for Cricket—his brothers Rugby, Golf and Fishing had changed their names by deed poll to Roger, Greg and Rod respectively, but Crick had kept his as an ironic tribute to their sports-mad father, now deceased). Crick glanced at the peeled paint and faded industrial grey carpet, then proceeded into the larger room that formed the hub of the Dark Office.

No ceiling lights were on, but the eerie blue glow from various monitors let Crick see that Bunt Wallac was slumped over his desk, an empty pizza box beside him. Had he slept there again? Andrea Mortocks startled Crick—she had been invisible until she crossed between him and a monitor. She didn't greet him, merely sat at her desk and adjusted the wireless headphones that covered her ears, tapping out a message on the company chat system instead.

Mortocks: *Have pushed the latest changes to staging, boss.*

Crick retreated to his own computer and clicked it into life.

Sema: *Thanks. You can keep going with the next round on dev if you like.*

Mortocks: *Already on it.*

Crick smiled, put on his headphones and settled into work. Small shufflings at the edge of his vision alerted him to the presence of other colleagues entering the office, but his noise-cancelling headphones let him enjoy his music undisturbed.

"Hey, hey, peoples!"

Crick cringed. Logo the designer swanned into the office, turning on the lights as he did so and bopping to the over-loud music emanating from the earphones hanging around his neck. Straight away Andrea tapped out a message to Crick on their private channel.

Mortocks: *If I have to put in a formal complaint about Logo one more time...!*

She left the threat hanging. Crick sent back a distressed-face emoji and shucked his headphones, standing to face Logo. He couldn't afford to sack the most brilliant designer he'd ever encountered, but Logo simply didn't adhere to the unspoken culture of the Dark Office. Garish colours battled for supremacy on his fitted, short-sleeved button up and his confident smile shone under his gold-framed aviators. Everyone else in the office wore black, except for Bunt, who compromised on navy jeans and t-shirts, usually unironed.

If that wasn't enough, Logo was loud—Crick considered emailing his headphones' manufacturer to tell them the true standard of testing should be this man, because while normal speech and the everyday beeps and taps of hardware were blocked out, Logo's voice could penetrate even the best Bose or Sony had to offer.

"How was your trip, Logo?" Christine, the soft-voiced peacekeeper of the office, piped up. "Family all well?" She was the Dark Office's front-woman—the client facing aspect. Enough technical knowledge to talk—well, message—the dev team, but with the social skills to communicate with outsiders. Crick blessed the day he'd hired her—no more client meetings for him! She tolerated Logo and usually toned him down to a modicum of quietness, thus preventing Andrea from either storming out or eviscerating their designer.

"It was great! Got back from Jakarta this morning! Family is same-old." Logo whipped off his aviators and grinned. "See you lot are being kept in the dark, as usual."

Christine groaned. Crick frowned. "It's called the Dark Office for a reason, Logo. What if Pleasance was here? We are vampire-friendly, remember?"

"Oh, Pleasance can't be hurt by fluros. Speaking of which, I thought you'd asked the landlord to upgrade to LEDs?"

"I did," Crick sighed. "He said there's a problem with the supplier. I'm waiting to hear back from him."

"If you're quite finished!" Andrea hissed, popping up from behind her screen. Crick glanced at his monitor, realising his star dev had been messaging with increased ire before being forced to speak out loud to get his attention. "Some of us are trying to work!" She returned her now furious attention to the screen.

Crick nodded at Christine, who moved to turn the lights down. Crick wished he could banish Logo into a corner, but the other employee's would see that as a sign of favour. No one was allowed a corner desk now, after a brief but intense argument had ensued. *We need more corners.* He sighed.

"Use your desk lamp, Logo," Crick instructed.

"Sure, man—whatever you say," the designer replied breezily and bounced to his desk, clicking his fingers to the beat of the latest song on his phone.

Crick surveyed the office quickly before Christine reached the switch. Jo wasn't present—their hours were so erratic Crick seldom saw the admin and HR manager, an androgynous human who claimed no gender and preferred the plural pronoun. Crick sighed. He'd have to compose an email to Jo about Logo, though the current crisis seemed to be averted.

Pleasance, their resident vampire, wasn't there either. Pleasance usually worked nights but occasionally stayed over-day. And Bunt was still asleep at his desk. Crick growled. Tolerant a boss he was, but this was taking it too far.

"Bunt!" He crossed from his row to the other. "Bunt!" No response. He could hear Andrea tapping away with alacrity, no doubt complaining about Crick's own lack of noise control.

The office fell into darkness just as Crick grasped Bunt's shoulder. Bunt still didn't respond

"Christine, turn the lights back on." Logo's normally cheerful voice sounded strange, disembodied. The fluoros flickered and resumed their cold glow. Logo stood on the other side of Bunt, a worried look on his face. Crick raised his eyebrows in annoyance.

"What is it?"

"Crick." Logo leaned forward and gently lifted one of Bunt's eyelids. "Crick, I think he's dead."

Andrea's tapping stopped. Crick looked at Logo and then down at Bunt. "Shit," he said. "He is too."

A STRANGE DEATH

Consumed by his own application programming interface (API). Dirk Samson typed the sentence then put his head in his hands. "What a strange way to die," he muttered. The backlit screen of his laptop cast an eerie light on his dark skin. "When are they going to get these damn lights fixed?" He frowned. As a coroner, he wasn't easily spooked, but the room was dark and the body on the slab next to him held an eerie life-like quality that most corpses had abandoned by the time they reached him.

"Just finish the report." He sighed and read over what he'd written so far. *White Caucasian male, age 33, found dead at his desk plugged into a virtual reality program. Cause of death: consciousness consumed by his own API.*

Forty minutes later he'd cross-checked and added sufficient technical notes to substantiate his verdict. He stretched, cracking his neck, and glanced at the body again. "Damn fool to be mucking about with virtual reality without safeguards."

"You talking to yourself, boss?" A Kiwi accent floated through the open door. "Or the corpse? Just be worried if they start answering."

Dirk chuckled. "Just myself, Teeps."

"Oh, well, that's a relief, bro. You almost finished in here?" Tipene edged into view, his burly frame tentative as usual. "Can I put the corpse back in the fridge?"

Dirk rubbed his eyes, hit save on his work and shut the laptop. "Yeah, go for it. I've lodged the death certificate. Hey, any word from maintenance on when they're fixing these lights?"

Tipene shrugged as he approached the wheeled table with the body. He drew up the sheet. "Some problem with the supplier, they said. I'll let you know if I hear anything, bro."

"Thanks." Dirk slid his laptop into his bag and left the morgue. He barely had to wait for a driverless car to roll up—there wasn't much traffic this late at night. On the way home he checked his personal emails but struggled to concentrate. Something bothered him about the developer's death—he just didn't know what. It bugged him the whole trip, so it was with relief he stepped through his front door to his warmly lit home filled with the scent of roast lamb.

"That you, honey?" His wife, Marigold, called out from the lounge room. "I put your dinner in the microwave!"

"Thank you!" He set his bag down on the kitchen table and heated his meal, savouring the smell of rosemary and potatoes. Dirk joined Marigold on the couch and kissed her cheek. She was watching the late news.

"Long day?" She smiled sympathetically, running a hand through her short grey hair.

"Got caught up with a VR death—some idiot running a program with no safeguards. Completely brain dead, body followed soon after. And they still haven't fixed the lights at work so I was sitting in the dark all evening."

Marigold frowned. "Didn't you say those were BluStop LEDs? I'm looking to buy shares in them. Local company."

"Mhm." Dirk chewed slowly, savouring the garlic-flavoured gravy. He swallowed. "I think so. We switched suppliers coz they were cheap, apparently."

"Hmph." The finance report came on. Marigold picked up her tablet and tapped the screen. "Gold's up, I'd better tell Violet to tighten the stops on her shares."

Dirk finished his dinner set his plate aside. "Delicious, honey. Sorry I wasn't home in time."

"Don't stress." Marigold patted his hand absently, still watching the TV. "I was watching a webinar. You'll be home early tomorrow night though, won't you? It's our anniversary."

Dirk gulped, then remembered he'd organised flowers and a dinner booking weeks ago and a laser light projection that said "Twenty-five years!" He smiled. "Of course, my dear. I'll be home by six."

DON'T MESS WITH THE ELDERY

Whispers at the other end of the phone line told Violet her call was having the desired effect. She grinned with geriatric glee, hitting the mute button and gesturing Marigold and Azalea to crowd around.

"They've forgotten to put me on hold, the duffers." She accepted her tea cup from Azalea and sipped delicately. It was an original Wedgewood set, beautifully painted in classic blue.

"Ginger biscuit?" Azalea offered. "Yes, it sounds like you've set the cat among the pigeons there." They listened to the tinny voices emitting from the phone.

"I spoke to her last time!"

"Yeah, and I thought you fobbed her off!"

"Old duck keeps coming back with more questions—she actually reads the reports and compares the figures to what we say in our emails!"

"Mmm, is this Lipton? It has a lovely, rounded taste. Marigold, you should try this," Violet advised.

"I'll stick to the Madura green leaf, thank you, my dear. Nothing beats a fresh pot of green tea." Marigold peered at the iPad in her hand. "Yes, he said in his last email that those insurance stocks saved us half the profits on the options he took out on our behalf. I'd hate to see what our losses would have been if we hadn't had them!"

"He's talking out of his arse," Violet responded succinctly. "The numbers don't add up and the dates he's talking about keep swapping around."

Azalea looked worried. "Do you really think they're dodgy? Maybe it's just a mistake."

"You're too trusting, Azalea." Marigold frowned.

"Give me the phone! I'll handle the old crone."

"Ooh, here he comes!" Violet placed her tea cup on the saucer with a gentle chink. She took the phone off speaker and answered the BluStop rep on the other end. "Yes, I'm here." She chuckled. "Oh, no, I haven't gone anywhere. Mhmm. Mhmm. Yes, that's why I called—the report I generated from the online portal is different to the one you sent me. Oh, yes, I had a clever computer friend help me with that—it's hard to keep up with all this new-fangled tech at my age." She referred to her tablet and flicked through several windows, firing off an email regarding a different stock and checking that the app recording the phone call was still running. "Oh, well, you check your numbers and let me know. If I don't hear from you by tomorrow I'll give you another tinkle. Hoo-roo!" She hung up.

"Crooked as a politician?" Marigold queried, peering over her bifocals.

"Definitely," Violet replied. She pursed her lips and drummed her fingers on her leg. "I doubt we'll get more satisfactory answers at the AGM next week. How can we prove that their financials are dodgy?"

"Pity we can't just pop in and have a look around," Azalea offered. "I've never seen a lightbulb factory. I imagine it would be all lit up."

"LEDs, not lightbulbs," Marigold corrected.

"I think we should pop in and have a squiz." Violet's fingers drummed faster. "But not during the day. We need to shine a light on this business."

Azalea coughed, breaking the awkward silence that followed. "Did you mean to say that?"

THE STARTUP VAMPIRE

The sun had long since set, but Pleasance automatically checked her handbag for the tube of zinc cream that lived there. Super senses, speed and strength were no help if solar radiation caused you to burn up faster than an unlucky witch on Spanish Inquisition bonfire night.

Pleasance sighed. She didn't moan like many of her fellow vampires. The angsty ones irritated her the most, with their gothic outfits and overdone eyeliner. They didn't help the image for more practical vampires like her. People in nightclubs would approach her for kinky favours—usually involving leather, biting and on occasion, glitter. Pleasance would stare them down until they slunk away, then walk all of her girlfriends home.

All it had taken was one mad biologist who'd binged on too many episodes of True Blood back in the day. Her version of "Hep-V" didn't actually create vampires—the victims didn't drink blood per se (unless they wanted to, but there were strict laws about that now). Instead, the stolen virus had spawned thousands of super-strong, super-fast, UV-averse, slow-aging infected who quickly banded together in a political lobby for rights before the vaccine had been developed.

Humans were now inoculated against Hep-V, but no cure had been engineered so the vampires remained. Pleasance took it in her stride—working nights as a developer meant the office was quiet. And she had plans; plans that didn't involve brooding in fancy dress and heavy makeup.

Nightclubs weren't on the agenda tonight. She strode through the deserted carpark as industrial fencing clinked in the breeze. The scent of chemicals from the nearby lighting factory made her nose twitch. A heavier clink caught her attention. A darker pool of shadows drew her eye. Several shapes became discernible as hissed whispers sounded clearly in Pleasance's ears.

"Shush, Violet, you're doing it wrong!"

"You bloody do it then! I told you to oil them before we came."

A third voice piped up. "I've got some coconut oil in my handbag—would that help?"

A pause. "Azalea, why have you got coconut oil in your handbag?"

"Why has she got her handbag? This is a covert operation!"

The voice belonging to the handbag responded primly. "I brought sandwiches in case we got peckish—what else was I going to carry them in? My picnic basket is too conspicuous."

Pleasance slunk closer, fascinated, using a skip bin as cover. The glow of a phone illuminated the faces of three women—they had to be seventy if they were a day—crouched around a set of bolt cutters.

The first woman spoke. "Azalea, we are conducting a raid, not having a picnic!"

The second woman, Violet, asked, "What kind of sandwiches?"

"Egg and spinach on rye."

"Forget the bloody sandwiches. Hand me that darn coconut oil to loosen up these bolt cutters."

Pleasance ghosted past. Tempted as she was to interfere, she needed to hurry. Tipene would only leave the morgue door unlocked until midnight. She left the would-be trespassers and raced along dark streets. The morgue adjoined the city hospital, tacked on at the rear like an embarrassed afterthought, built in a utilitarian fashion where the rest of the facility was architecturally streamlined.

The door was ajar, as Tipene had promised. Pleasance slipped inside then swiped her stolen pass bracelet to gain access to the inner sanctum. The shelf holding Bunt's body slid easily from the chilly embrace of the industrial refrigerator and Pleasance placed the AI storage chip into the trepanned port at the back of Bunt's head. While that uploaded his consciousness she sat at one of the computer terminals and hacked into the system. In the time it took to reactivate Bunt's brainwaves she had the death certificate copied and erased all trace of her access.

A groan emitted from Bunt's pale lips. Pleasance shut down the terminal and wiped everything down for fingerprints before she wrapped a robe around Bunt and hauled his no-longer-corpse over her shoulder. She shoved the shelf back into the fridge, closing the door with a slight *whuff* of air. Speeding through the dark streets, the heavy body no hindrance to her vampiric strength, they were safe back at the office by the time Bunt started twitching.

She propped him on his chair and stuck an IV in his arm, reintroducing fluids as he slowly reanimated. While he recovered, Pleasance logged into her computer and coded.

"So it worked?" Bunt slurred, head lolling.

"Would we be having this conversation if it hadn't?"

"Cer-tiff-i-cate?"

"Already emailed to you. Go ahead and lodge the claim. I expect half the money in my account by the end of the month."

Bunt grunted agreement.

"I suppose you need help getting home?"

Bunt managed to grasp the squeezy-bottle of water and take a sip. "Caan't go home. Got place 'ganised. Fake naame. Gimme… few more minutes. 'll get a car."

"Take your time—I've got a ton of work to catch up on." She typed while Bunt clutched the arms of his chair, upper body swaying gently. Pleasance wondered what he intended to do with his life insurance payout. She knew what *she* wanted to do.

As if reading her mind (*not* a vampiric ability), Bunt mumbled, "So whaa you gonnna do wi'ya casssh?"

Pleasance didn't take her eyes from the screen. "Got an eye on a few tech startups. Going to invest then take a nap."

"A naap?"

"A decade or two. I'll get a proxy to manage my shares." The problem with being a young vampire was you still had to work, and while vampires had rights, they certainly weren't always welcome. Money would improve that situation.

Bunt humphed, whether in surprise or because he was impressed, she didn't know. He lurched to his feet like the proverbial Frankenstein's monster, yanking out the IV line. "I'mma goood now," he slurred.

"Sure," said Pleasance. She pulled out the final weapon in her Mary Shelly arsenal—an epipen. Stabbing Bunt's leg, she watched her colleague straighten and gasp.

"Ow!"

"That should get you home. Have a good rest, and keep hydrated. Take your vitamins."

"I know—it was my plan," he scowled, looking around the Dark Office, its array of multi-coloured monitor lights like silent sentinels. "Won't miss this place."

He staggered up the stairs, and Pleasance returned to her desk and carried on as if nothing had happened.

WHISTLEBLOWER

The air was thick with the smell of hot weetbix; it misted through the cracks in the building. Nick always regretted the location of his workplace at this time of the afternoon—the Seventh Day Adventists had an enthusiasm for cereal, so much so it had led them to invest in factories churning out the stuff, and one of those factories was unfortunately the next plot over from Nick's work.

Did I miss the bit in the Bible that went, 'And the Lord sayeth, thou shalt sow the wheat, harvest the wheat, turn the wheat into compressed bricks for breakfast cereal at 3pm each day'? It was possible. Most of Nick's Religious Education classes had consisted of him using a wooden ruler to play cricket in the chapel or going for 'spiritual walks' with mates—as long as they carried a prayer book the chaplain had been fine with it.

Still, the weetbix smell was a good reminder that he was late to the company-wide briefing being held in Warehouse A. He hurried down the hallway, swift footsteps dulled by the industrial carpet. The latch snicked shut as the office door closed behind him. If asked what he was doing, he'd say he'd been asking to grab a report for his line manager. Never mind that all reports could be remotely accessed and his line manager was never seen without a tablet. *Some reports are too sensitive for that.* He clutched the tiny data card and shoved it into his pants pocket, then grabbed a couple of tissues from the receptionist's desk as he hurtled past, wadding them and bundling them into the pocket as well.

He slipped in through the service door of Warehouse A, just in time to catch the middle of the CEO's uninspiring speech about how mediocre the company was for representation.

"We don't rate highly in the diversity stakes compared to our contemporaries. When the economic downturn came, we had to let a heap of people go, and the ones we let go were… the diverse people."

Nick's jaw dropped. His eyes bulged and shot from side to side. Was no one going to react?

Most of the other workers sat slumped in their chairs, glassy eyed, slack-mouthed, no doubt thinking about the number of minutes until the free sausage sizzle started. Nick shook his head, catching the eye of Shuri, the head electrical engineer, who grimaced as if to say, *welcome to my every day.*

Nick rubbed the bridge of his nose, more and more convinced he was doing the right thing.

The CEO finished his rousing oration by declaring that Blustop would continue to provide top quality LEDs to the market whilst delivering excellent returns to their shareholders. A desultory applause followed once his audience woke enough to realise he was done, with a more sincere effort at clapping once the site manager declared the sausage sizzle was to begin.

"You not eating either, Nick?" Shuri found him loitering by the forklifts, nursing a half-drunk can of soft drink.

"Huh? Oh, no—not hungry. You?" Nick noticed Shuri had a determined set to her shoulders. She had never lacked confidence (and boy had she needed it in a warehouse of blokes who were set in their ways) but this evening she carried extra steel in her posture.

"I'm having dinner later—celebrating." She smiled conspiratorially, white teeth gleaming against her dark skin.

"Oh?"

"Been offered a job with GlowSteel. Getting away from this dump. Be nice to work somewhere that doesn't remind me of a Trump rally back in the teens." Shuri rolled her eyes. "You should get out too, Nick. This place ain't healthy."

Nick froze, unsure. His relief that Shuri was leaving (she was a brilliant engineer—wasted at BluStop) ebbed when he considered the fact she might be fishing for information. *You're being paranoid! No one knows what you're up to!* "I'm really happy for you," he mumbled. "I'm settled here though—it's a good job." There—nothing too obvious. He didn't wax on about company values (would have sounded fake), nor did he slam the business and lay himself open for suspicion. Lazy self-interest was the smartest cover.

Shuri shrugged. "You'll never go anywhere here. I'll miss ya, Nick." She turned on her hell and threaded through the crowd. Nick watched her go, then made an effort to mingle with his co-workers, laughing at the story of old Damo chasing pigeons in the warehouse with his air rifle, counting the minutes until knock-off time, nauseated by the smell of cheap supermarket sausages.

Finally everyone was gone and he slipped back up to his office—a rickety upstairs room overlooking the warehouse floor, very different to the mahogany desked boardrooms and wide-windowed offices of the main admin building where he had been earlier. *And that ain't even where half the money goes!* He copied the data from the card he had stolen earlier then shoved it back in his pocket, re-wadding the tissues on top. Beginning a file transfer from his laptop, he fidgeted as he waited.

The office door burst in. Nick started. "Mr Lucas!"

The site manager ambled over to Nick's messy desk. Two factory security guards flanked him, thickset features menacing. "Working late, Nick?"

Sweat broke out in Nick's armpits, though he managed to keep his voice calm. "Just sending off a few emails." He minimised the web transfer window and tried to smile blithely. "Can I do something for you?"

Mr Lucas considered Nick for a moment, a half-smile on his face, reminiscent of the school bully right before he swung a punch. Then he lifted Nick's laptop off the desk and smashed it over his knee.

"Holy shit!" Nick rocked back in his chair, almost going over. He saved himself by hooking a foot on the desk leg. "What the hell?"

"I think you know, Nick." Mr Lucas' smile was gone, replaced with a sneer. The tinkle of laptop shards surrounded the crunch of the computer hitting the wooden floorboards. "Selling out on us? BluStop can't have some smarmy little do-gooder squealing. Who were you sending the files to?"

Nick gripped the edge of the desk, willing himself not to bring his hands anywhere near his pockets. "Don't know what you're talking about, Mr Lucas." *I'm a dead man. Shit shit shit, I'm a dead man.*

One of the security thugs cracked his knuckles. Nick didn't wait. He lunged sideways, putting a shoulder through the side window that looked out over the warehouse, feeling hot blood streak his arms.

"Get him!"

His heart pounded in his ears. Sensing rather than seeing, he knew the security guards were millimetres behind him when he dived like a rugby forward desperate to score the deciding try. He hit the crossbar of one of their loading cranes, scrabbling with slippery hands.

Shouting ensued, but Nick didn't wait. He hauled himself up and clambered along the strut.

"You can't stay up there forever, Nick!" Mr Lucas yelled.

He didn't plan on it. He intended to get down as fast as possible and beat the security guards to the door. It was his only chance.

Something whacked the strut near his head. More missiles rained up at him. The security guards were emulating old Damian, the forklift driver who hurled objects at the pigeons who dared to fly into the warehouse in search of shelter. Nick felt confident he could survive the battery, then a pop sounded and his leg jerked in agony. He looked around.

Mr Lucas had found old Damo's illegal ancient air rifle, nemesis of any feathered creature who dared brave the onslaught of empty cardboard tubes. Nick pushed off from the horizontal strut to the crane's upright, knowing he needed something between him and the gun, but his injured leg failed.

He fell, wishing he'd left early with Shuri.

Wishing he hadn't tried to be so clever.

He'd hoped to send the data from on site in order to pretend it was a natural leak.

He failed.

He hit the ground.

EVEN LIZARD OVERLORDS HAVE THEIR LIMITS

Marguerite Hoffman extended her claws just enough to scratch the terrible itch her scales suffered every afternoon. In her guise as a middle-aged professional woman, she wore the synthetic skin that every reptilian overlord wore in public. But it didn't agree with her natural oils, and she hated it.

Why couldn't I have been assigned to a world where we didn't hide our presence? Earth was troublesome, and Marguerite was fed up with the scheming and all the cloaked machinations that overlording from the shadows required. *And to be assigned to one of the most boring industries on this planet, too!* Her colleagues manipulated politicians; they monitored the secrets of cutting-edge science. She assessed insurance claims.

Ughh! "What's next?" she enquired of her assistant, Tony, a bright young man sporting tightly curled black hair with hot pink tips. He handed her a tablet and smiled, teeth brilliant against dark skin.

"Death claim, bit of a weird one—something to do with being hooked up to a VR program. Been referred to you because the body went missing right after the death certificate was filed."

Marguerite was hardly listening. She swivelled her office chair to stare out of the floor to ceiling plate glass windows, longing to be out there in the sunshine, to shed the rubbery skin that choked her scales, to work hours that suited her and never, *ever,* look at another insurance claim.

"It's fine, let it go through," she told Tony.

"Let it go through?" Her assistant's astonishment was plain.

"Yes!" Marguerite snapped. She scratched her wrist hard, feeling the synthetic skin tear. "I'm the head underwriter, and I say let it go through!"

"Okay!" Tony's brows went high and he sounded alarmed. Marguerite knew the natural red of her eyes must be glowing through the contact lenses, and she struggled to calm down.

A knock at the door broke the tension, followed by the bouncing entrance of Daffyd, a flirtatious underwriter with a singsong voice and a dashing smile. "Hi Marguerite, you wanted to see me? Oh, hey Tony, how's things?" Daffyd winked at Tony and Marguerite envied the casual cheeriness of her colleague.

"H-hi Daffyd." Tony blushed and stumbled over his words. "I'm g-good, what's been happening?"

"Crushing buckets, my friend, crushing buckets. Hey, you coming to drinks after work?"

"Ah, I can't—family thing." Tony looked as if he would rather cancel his entire family's existence for the chance to go out for drinks with Daffyd, and Marguerite wondered at the complex courting rituals of humans.

"If you two are quite done," she interrupted, feeling old and tired and out of touch with the slang and the flirting of the planet's natives. *Maybe if I lived in the world, rather than assessing humans from behind all this paperwork, I would understand.*

"Sorry, Marguerite," Daffyd grinned, unabashed. "What did you want?"

She stood, still scratching absently at her wrist. The motion drew the eyes of the two men.

"Er… got a nasty bit of eczema there, Marguerite," Tony blurted. "You want to get some cream for that?"

Marguerite's patience snapped. Tiny pops signalled spines bursting through the fake skin on her back. Her business jacket would hide them for now, but she dared not turn. "Do you like the view from this office, Daffyd?" She gestured behind her, voice as cool as the greenish blood that ran through her veins.

"Sure, it's great." Daffyd nodded at the panorama visible through the windows. The river wend its way around the CBD, sparkling in the sunlight except where tall buildings cast long shadows, and bridges arched and spiked their way over the river's span.

"Good. It's yours." Marguerite closed her laptop and picked up her designer handbag. *Ridiculous, the things I've had to spend money on to keep up appearances.*

"I'm sorry?" Daffyd's normally easy-going expression was beset by confusion.

"Don't be," Marguerite responded, unclipping her work access pass from her lanyard and placing it on the desk. "While I don't have the authority to promote you, I've written a very nice letter of recommendation and they'd be fools to pass you up as the next head-underwriter."

Tony demanded, "Are you quitting?"

"Marguerite, if you're not feeling good, take the afternoon off," Daffyd implored.

"I'm feeling perfectly well." This was not strictly accurate, but soon she would be free. As if summoned by the thought, her frill edged out from under her permed wig.

"Ah, Marguerite…?" Even Daffyd looked unnerved.

"Don't stress, gentlemen." Marguerite strode passed her colleagues to her office door. "I just emailed my letter of resignation, and I'm taking the rest of the day as sick leave." Her tail lashed with excitement, disturbing the fabric of her Hilary Clinton-esqe pantsuit but she didn't care. She was finally acting upon her long suppressed desire. Let the consequences be what they would.

It wasn't until the elevator door had dinged closed, and the office door had been shut securely, that Tony and Daffyd stared at each other. "Did we just see… what I think we saw?" Tony ventured.

"I don't know what we just saw," Daffyd declared. "But I'm thinking after work isn't soon enough for that drink. You coming?"

Tony nodded fervently, and decided that whiskey was the only appropriate beverage at a time like this. He didn't want beer that came in a green bottle, or any drink that was remotely the shade of anything that might remind him of the skin of a lizard.

FINGERPRINTS AND FILES

"You need money for *what?* Bail? Mum, what the hell do you need bail money *for?*"

"Darling, it sounds worse than it is. I don't want to call your father because you know how his heart is, but I seem to have been arrested for murder."

Hangsu's screech of "*WHAT?*" would have been heard up and down the street if she hadn't automatically modulated it to a safer decibel level—safer because she didn't want to wake her baby and deal with the whinging rage that came from a small human who hadn't had enough sleep but refused to acknowledge it.

"Anyway, darling, I also wanted to let you know I can't babysit this afternoon. I'm waiting for my lawyer to arrive. I'm terribly sorry—will you be alright?"

Hangsu felt the rising panic that came with sudden changes of plan, but hid the tell-tale squeak from her voice. "Of course. We'll just go to the park or something. Just let me know if you need anything else, Mum."

"Just the bail money for now, darling. If you could transfer that to me that would really help. Now don't you worry—this will all blow over and we'll do something nice on the weekend. Hooroo!"

Hangsu stared at the phone after her mother hung up. The cheerful image of her family smiled back at her, but Hangsu couldn't bring herself to return the cheesy grins. *What in the heck has mum gotten herself into now?*

She was unable to dwell on her mother's predicament, however. Distracted by her mother's call, her toddler had opened the forbidden pantry door to engage in her favourite sport of can stacking. With the silent precision of a child who knows they are doing something they shouldn't, her daughter chose that moment to topple an impressively high tower of tins. The cans crashed to the wooden floor, much to her toddler's delighted shout of, "Oh, no!" An outraged wail signalled the awakening of her baby, and Hangsu clenched her fists in an effort not to scream. With the prospect of no babysitting for the afternoon, she wanted to cry.

She took a deep breath. "Come on," she helped her daughter scoop up the scattered tins of baked beans and spaghetti. "You build another tower while mummy gets your brother. Then we're going to get sushi." She ordered a driverless car as she grabbed a nappy bag and her e-reader. It was close enough to her toddler's naptime that a drive would put her to sleep. There was no chance of settling both children at home at the same time. *Juggling naptimes is the worst!* Hangsu retrieved her red-faced, bawling son just as the car pulled up outside, bundling them out the door with considerable effort. ("More beans!" her daughter screamed, clinging to the doorframe. "More beeeeaaaaaannnss!")

Battling with the children to get out the door, she avoided looking at her neighbour, who was acting out some sort of ritualistic looking dance in her front yard. Deleria was a bit odd, to put it kindly. Frazzled hair and copious amounts of jewellery, she always seemed to be engaged in drama. Right now she seemed too absorbed to notice Hangsu's heroic efforts of placing baby in the waiting car *(thank whoever that you can order cars with baby seats)* while holding onto her daughter's wrist. The toddler fought with tiger-like tenacity to escape her mother's torturous grip, all the while hollering at the top of her lungs.

Finally, both children in car and secure, Hangsu straightened to see neighbour Deleria peering over the fence. "Naptime, you know," Hangsu offered lamely, not having the energy to explain further.

Fortunately Deleria's judgement was not concerned with the children's behaviour. "Wonderful lungs, that girl of yours," she proclaimed. "Such passion. With that kind of vocal projection she could be an *artiste* like me."

"Er, thank you." Hangsu could still hear the wonderful lungs through the closed car door, now screaming in chorus with her son.

"Send her to me when you wish to begin her education! We shall foster her creativity. But for now, adieu." Deleria curtseyed. "I must perform the next chapter of my novel—Sir Randolph is meeting the Duchess at the ball." She swirled and Hangsu noticed for the first time her neighbour's get up—like something out of a Jane Austen drama, and totally inappropriate for the humid weather.

Shaking her head, Hangsu climbed into the car and tapped in the destination—via several freeway loops. The rumble of the wheels on bitumen cast their spell on the overtired kids—both toddler and baby were passed out by the time they reached their goal.

All her mum-friend's raved about this place. It had only been open a few weeks but already business was booming. Coffee, sushi, healthy wraps. Water and babychinos were free with any purchase if you had a reusable bottle or keep-cup. It was near a really good park with a fenced playground, lots of shady trees and plenty of that chip-rubber matting that was soft on kids' feet without the filth and inconvenience of chip bark or sand. Often busy but never over-crowded, the drive-through sushi joint was run by a cheerful middle-aged proprietor who personally came out to take orders.

"Call me Margy," she said to Hangsu the first time they'd visited. Margy had vivid green tattoos on her wrists and neck, peeking out from her loose long-sleeve button up blouse. Hangsu's daughter had pointed and said "snake lady" the first time she had seen them. Hangsu had been mortified and admonished her toddler, but Margy had just laughed and said, "Actually they are lizard scales, pet. You can call me lizard lady if you like."

Hangsu reflected her daughter would probably be sad to have missed the 'lizard lady', but there was no way she was waking her as the driverless car trundled into the queue. She keyed the window down as Margy came up to the car, smiling cheerfully.

"Hello, Hangsu! Little ones asleep? Gosh, they are precious."

Hangsu smiled wryly. "Especially when they are asleep."

Margy nodded sympathetically. "Extra shot in your soy latte? No charge—you look like you need it."

About to decline, then remembering she had no babysitter to give her a reprieve that afternoon, Hangsu accepted gratefully, saying, "But of course I'll pay for it."

"Don't be silly, pet. Now give me your water bottle and I'll fill it up. Are you having some sushi or a wrap today?" She ambled alongside the car as it inched forward around the semi-circular drive.

Hangsu ordered tuna-avocado rolls, with salmon nigiri as a treat. No children awake meant she didn't have to share. Margy tapped everything into her tablet and accepted Hangsu's payment—minus the cost of the extra shot.

"You're too kind, Margy."

"Not at all, pet. You take care now." The 'lizard lady' waved Hangsu off and trundled back to the next car in line, seeming to relish the hot sun burning down. Hangsu shook her head and closed the car window, retreating into the air-conditioned peace of the car. She watched the cheerful sushi chefs through the building's glass walls. They rolled and diced and seared fresh sushi while the barista methodically worked through orders. It was unlike any other drive through—all light and sunshine and older employees, some of whom, if you peered closely enough, could be seen sporting the strange green scale tattoos. *Maybe it's a gang thing,* Hangsu thought, though the amicable collective of hospitality workers seemed the farthest thing from a gang as she could imagine.

A lean man with salt-and-pepper hair acted as runner, delivering the paper-wrapped sushi along with Hangsu's coffee and her re-filled water bottle. "Enjoy your lunch," he winked, nodding at the sleeping children. Hangsu directed the car to idle in a nearby street, glad the solar panels on the roof made this kind of an indulgence guilt-free, and tried not to scoff her sushi, reminding herself that she didn't have to guard every bite from small hands.

Sipping her coffee, her mind returned to the drama that had unfolded earlier. How had her mum been arrested for murder? *Can't call dad. Hmm, I bet one of mum's investor friends know what's going on.* She dialled Violet. No answer. Allowing another draft of hot caffeine to infuse her brain, she tried her mother's other friend, Azalea.

"Yes? Hello?"

"Azalea? It's Hangsu, Marigold's daughter. How are you?"

A certain hesitation told she this had been the right number. "Oh, I'm fine, thank you. How are you? How are the children?"

"We're fine. Azalea, I'm sorry to bother you, but do you know anything about what's going on with mum?"

A silence so poignant filled Hangsu's ear, and for a moment she feared the line had disconnected. She opened her mouth to say, "Are you still there?"

Azalea burst out, "She didn't do it! I know she didn't—we were with her the entire time! There may have been a few moments where I couldn't see her because I'd stopped to rebalance the picnic basket but she couldn't have done what they said she did in that time! It was all so horrible I almost threw up my egg and spinach sandwich. There was blood all over the floor!"

What the...? "Azalea, what are you talking about? What happened?"

Bit by bit, she drew the story out of Azalea. A break in to investigate a financially dodgy company. Finding a body on the factory floor. Her mother panicking and dropping her tablet. The police showing up at her mum's house, arresting her for murder. "They said they had her fingerprints on the corpse. But she never touched it! I tried to pick up the broken pieces—you know I hate to leave a mess."

"Thanks, Azalea. I'll take it from here." Hangsu interrupted the babble and rubbed her temples. *Oh mum. This is out of control!*

"Oh, Hangsu, one more thing. I forgot about it in the fuss but when I tried to pick up your mother's tablet I seemed to have picked up a data card that isn't hers. It has lots of reports on it. Do you think I should tell the police?"

Hangsu's son opened his eyes and said, "Mama?" Automatically, she handed him a rice cracker and his sippy cup of water. She calculated he would munch in peace for ten minutes before flipping from cute bubba to wailing banshee.

"Stay where you are, Azalea. I'm coming to get that card."

MARRIED INTO THE FAMILY

Tony straightened his bowtie and stepped into the banquet room. The wedding reception was in full swing; guests crisscrossing the floor to mingle, champagne lubricating social interactions for better and worse. Tony sighed in relief—no one would notice that he'd disappeared after the ceremony to see Daffyd home. His poor date was sick. He had insisted on coming to the ceremony but accepted that he was too ill to handle Tony's boisterous extended family after a few drinks.

"Good evening, dear Anthony." His sister-in-law Deleria swept up, outfitted as if for a masque ball. She twiddled the stick holding her extravagant cat mask, then generously held out her free hand for him to kiss.

"Hi Dee." Eccentric as she was, Tony liked Deleria. He thought she was batty as a Carpathian cave but she didn't give him grief about being gay or ask him about his job prospects, unlike the rest of his incredibly straight-laced family. He bowed over her hand, booping it with his nose rather than his lips. "Nice mask."

She seemed satisfied with that. "Did you know cats evolved to be addictive? That's why people end up acquiring more and more."

"Is that so?" Tony nabbed two glasses from a nearby table and caught the eye of a waitress. She filled them with bubbles, or—as Tony liked to say—false bravado and lowered inhibitions.

Tony held a glass out to Deleria. "Drink, m'lady?"

"Why, thank you, darling boy."

Tony led them to an deserted table in the corner—the table's occupants evidently having realised they'd been seated in the least desirable spot and fanned out to insert themselves in more salubrious social circles. "You and Derrick having a nice time?" He couldn't see his brother—he was no doubt extolling his latest courtroom exploits to an agog crowd of cousins.

"Oh, yes." Deleria lowered her voice. "Darling Derrick is collecting intel—we're on a mission, spying for the government."

"Excellent." Tony nodded. "So the latest book is coming along well?"

Deleria beamed at him. "It certainly is, my dear boy." An independent author, Deleria acted out scenes from her novels. *My writing is an immersive process,* she would say.

"So what's Derrick's cover?" Tony asked, already knowing the answer. His brother adored Deleria, humoured her drama, but never participated.

"A high profile barrister. Perfect for an occasion such as this, darling." It was always a lawyer. Probably because Derrick's actual occupation was that, and he never missed an opportunity at a social occasion to wax lyrical about his courtroom prowess.

As if summoned, Derrick wandered up, tipsy and jovial, accompanied by a lady Tony didn't recognise. "Tony! Good to see you, brother! I was just telling Uncle Ian about my latest case—proved an old lady innocent of murder! Brilliant work, on my part—got evidence from the daughter that my client's fingerprints had been lifted from her tablet and planted on the corpse. And I linked the murder to dodgy dealings by the company! There's going to be a whole inquiry now."

"Nice work," Tony said weakly, overwhelmed by the informational barrage. "And who's your friend?" He attempted to include the lady out of politeness.

"Oh!" Derrick seemed to remember himself. "This is Christine. She's a developer. She's single." He waggled his eyebrows suggestively and sauntered away.

Christine waved awkwardly. "Hi."

"Lady Deleria Fantasmagoria." Dee launched into her own introduction. "Married into the family. Maiden name Rokarolanov, of the Siberian Rokarolanovs. Darling Derrick is my husband. I have energy stones for magic spells if you need them."

"Hi, I'm Tony, Derrick's brother. I'm gay and I have a boyfriend." Tony shrugged and smiled.

"Cool," Christine said hesitantly. "Do you know where the bathrooms are?"

Tony pointed helpfully. Christine grabbed his glass of champagne and downed it before making a beeline for the toilets. Tony chuckled and relaxed back into his chair, looking at Deleria. "Energy stones?"

Deleria produced an old-fashioned square tin with a lid. She tipped out several black lumps and held them out for Tony to inspect.

"This is coal," Tony said skeptically.

"I know! If you add them to fire you release energy!" She declared triumphantly. "I know a man who refined his eyebrows to great effect using them in a spell."

Tony had to laugh. Of all his family, Deleria was his favourite.

BACK IN THE DARK

Crick flicked the switch and the new LEDs came to life immediately. He heaved a sigh and promptly switched them off again. "Well that was a tumultuous mix of frustrating and exhausting," he told Christine.

"It's done now," she said consolingly.

"Not sure why you bother," Logo chimed in from his sprawled position in a chair. "You prefer to keep us all in the dark anyway. We don't even have a vampire working for us anymore."

Crick pretended not to hear. He filed the invoice for the new lights and shot an email to his bookkeeper stating that the purchase of the old LEDs would have to be written off since the supplier company was in receivership thanks to criminal prosecution.

He moved back out to the reception area. Jo was actually in the office for once, and monopolizing the 3D printer.

"What are you printing?" Crick asked.

"Replacement for Bunt," Jo answered shortly. "Operation Body Builder. It's the answer to every HR manager's dreams."

"Er… I suppose I did say we need more staff."

"Yep. And this way we just create them ourselves. Andrea's working on the AI component right now."

Crick considered having androids for employees. *Wait, won't they simply be tools?* "Why bother make them humanoid?"

"Easier for collaboration with Logo and Christine. Besides, if we need a developer to attend a client meeting we need a body in the room. Andrea refuses, so unless you want to go back to talking to clients…?"

"Fair enough," Crick replied hastily. "Clients probably won't even notice."

Jo grinned. "Not by the time we're finished with them. Bunt 2.0 and Pleasance 2.0 will even have some characteristics of their predecessors."

"That's creepy," Crick muttered, and left Jo to it.

TURNING POINTS TALES

"Move, Jew!"

The blow sent Adi stumbling but she regained her balance by grabbing the door frame. She glared at the portly cook then dipped her eyes when her bully lifted an iron soup ladle. Adi fled the kitchen.

"I don't know why Silva keeps you," Adi hissed once out of earshot, cradling her bruised arm. She did know—the Gaul was an excellent chef, turning out elaborate feasts with originality and flair. Now that Silva had returned a celebrated hero from Judea he threw banquets on a regular basis.

Adi sighed. She missed the quiet days before the General's return.

"Adi? Are you alright?"

Adi's head shot up. "Want do you want?"

Gaius' face was a picture of concern. She hadn't seen him much in the year since Silva's return—his boyish good looks had matured, his blonde curls darkened but kept neat. "Did someone hit you?"

Adi smiled crookedly. When *wasn't* the cook lashing out at someone? "I'm fine. Nothing for you to concern yourself with." She spoke politely but kept her words clipped. She turned to go.

"Adi." Gaius put out a hand but didn't touch her. "I need to talk to you."

"So talk." She didn't want to be accused of loitering with him. Plenty of other slaves had dalliances, but she remained aloof.

Gaius glanced down the corridor. Noise and bustle from the kitchen warned that someone could come along at any moment. Adi shifted her weight in agitation. "Not here," he said. "Will you meet me by the fountain after supper?"

"No." She worked long days as a slave. She wasn't sacrificing sleep to talk to another slave that she didn't even like.

"Please," Gaius begged. "It's about Masada. It's about Gwyn."

Adi stiffened. They hadn't spoken of Gwyn since the day Gaius had led them from the bowels of the fortress through smoke and soldiers. They'd told his General of the Sicarii's mass suicide. After hearing their tale, Silva ordered Gaius to take Adi and the other survivors back to Rome to be slaves in his household.

"Please meet me." Gaius gazed at her. She couldn't tell what he was thinking.

"Fine." She turned abruptly and fled.

Quiet reigned in the courtyard garden. The full moon sprinkled its light into a thousand pieces upon the burbling fountain. The nymphs that decorated the marble plinths and elegantly carved benches hid their faces in the shadows. Adi relaxed in the warm spring air.

"Your Latin is so much better now." Gaius spoke softly as he emerged from behind the lemon trees.

Adi tensed but stayed sitting by the fountain. "Thank you." She wanted to reply bitingly but that would have been churlish. Gaius had taught her his language—she owed him thanks for that at least. "What did you want to say to me?"

He hesitated. He had a thick green leaf from a lemon tree in his fingers. He folded it and the membranes snapped. Adi waited, irritation creeping up on her. "I want to know what you know of Gwyn. We never talked much about her, back at Masada or on the ship."

I was too busy mourning my people. Adi rubbed her eyes. "It was years ago now. Does it matter?" Despite her words, the chance to speak of her friend made her tremble.

"It matters to me." Gaius sat abruptly on the edge of the fountain. Adi leant away.

"She came from a village near the Salt Sea," Adi said. "Our men had… gone there to get supplies."

"I saw the village," Gaius said. His eyes locked with hers. "It was looted and burned."

Adi sagged. She had known the Sicarii raided and killed fellow Jews to ensure their own survival. "They found Gwyn there, brought her back, and she prophesised the Roman attack. Then she lived with us while we prepared for the siege. She… warned me to hide in the water cisterns when the time came. I don't know how she knew." Her voice choked. "I didn't want to die. I should have. I should have let Joshua kill me and Auntie and the children. Better than becoming a slave. My parents would be ashamed. I don't keep the traditions. I was glad when that fever came and took the boys, but angry that it left Maria and me. I should kill myself but I still want to live." Tears spilled over and ran down her cheeks.

She felt arms around her and she sobbed harder. Gaius rocked her gently and murmured, "I'm sorry," into her hair. Adi gradually pulled herself under control and stiffened. Gaius sat back. "I'm sorry," he said. "Gwyn wanted me to save you. I'm sorry Silva made you a slave but it's not so bad. It's a good house and you have food and clothes."

Adi sniffed and made a face. "I'm still a slave. And a Jew. That makes me dirt to the other slaves." She wiped her eyes and said, "Was that it? Is there anything else you want to know?" The humiliation of crying in front of him burned after keeping her thoughts and feelings hidden for so long.

"Maybe," he replied. "I don't know. I could tell you what I know of her, what she said to me, but it's late. Will you come tomorrow night?"

Excitement and confusion surged inside her chest. She shouldn't—it was weak, dwelling on the past, trying to dissect the strange events that led to her people's downfall. But to break the monotony of life in this cluttered, noisy household, to remember a time when she'd been hopeful and free—that was worth another late night.

"Tomorrow," she agreed.

The next night, and the next, and then another after that. They talked about the mysterious girl who had changed their lives at Masada.

"The thing she had," Gaius explained, "the amulet—it persuaded people. That's how she convinced me to help her escape. We walked all the way to En Gedi." Adi couldn't be sure, but she thought he blushed in the dark. The moon was waning so the light wasn't as strong. Some nights they missed—too busy or too tired—but every few days they would sit by the fountain as the summer wore on, and talk.

Tonight he was late. Adi sat awhile, then paced by the lemon trees. She brushed a branch and a yellow leaf dropped to the paving.

"Adi, I'm sorry I'm late. Silva sent for me." Gaius strode into the courtyard. His blonde hair was freshly trimmed and he wore a new tunic. He set a lantern on a plinth and sat by the fountain. Adi sat next to him. Gaius jumped up. She looked at him, surprised.

"What's the matter?" Why was he so agitated? Was he in trouble? He was a shadow to Silva in the day—surely that was the sign of a favourite?

Gaius cracked his knuckles. "I have something important to say. You know tomorrow is Silva's birthday?"

"The whole household knows, Gaius," Adi pointed out drily. "I've spent the last week polishing plates and vases till my hands ache." She softened her statement with a half smile.

"Oh. Of course. Sorry." He was out of knuckles to crack so clasped his hands together and faced Adi directly. "He called me into his study before."

"Enter," Silva called. Gaius walked in, nervous and excited. He thought he knew what was going to happen and was prepared. "Ah, Gaius. I'll make this brief. You've repaid your indenture and been a faithful servant so I'm going to manumit you tomorrow before my birthday feast."

"Thank you, sir." Gaius bowed. "I'm most grateful."

A gracious nod. "Now it is customary to grant a gift or boon upon manumission, to set up a freedman in his new life. You will take my nomen, Flavius, and always be considered a part of my family. Now what will it be? A shop? Some property?"

Gaius took a deep breath. "A boon, if you would, sir. I would ask the freedom of the two Jewish girls from Masada." He stood still, waiting to hear his master's reply.

Silva's brow furrowed. "The two Jewish girls? Whatever for? Weren't there some other children as well? Or did we sell them?"

"They died, sir. There was a fever just before you came home from Judea. And the old woman died before we reached Rome. There are just the two girls left—the older is nineteen, the younger eleven."

Silva raised his eyebrows. "And what do you want these two girls for?" An awkward pause hung over them.

Gaius forged ahead. "I want to marry the elder, Adi, and adopt the younger, Maria."

A longer pause. Silva sat back in his chair and considered Gaius. "Not gold. Not property or a business. Two slaves."

"Their freedom, sir, and your permission to marry Adi and adopt Maria." Gaius struggled not to fidget. He wiggled his toes in his sandals and looked at the writing tools on Silva's desk. Stylus, ink, parchment, sand. Would they spell out his wish, or had he just lost his chance?

Silva raised his eyebrows again and spread his hand wide. "If that's what you want, lad, though I daresay you're making a mistake. Wives and daughters cost money, I should know. You'd be better off setting yourself up in a business and then getting a family the old-fashioned way."

Gaius fought to keep the smile from his face. "Thank you, sir, I appreciate it, sir." He watched as Silva waived the scribe over to make out the papers. Silva signed and pressed his seal into the wax. "I'll present these tomorrow, but in the meantime, congratulations." His face was rueful. "What will you do?"

"My uncle has a barge business in Ostia," Gaius said. "He's unwell so I'll take over." He didn't say how lucky it was that Silva was freeing him before his uncle died. As much as he hated the molesting old bastard, he was prepared to make amends with a dying man for the sake of an inheritance that his sister deserved. He was now free to do that, though it turned his stomach.

"Very well. Good luck with it. See you before the feast tomorrow." Silva waved Gaius out. Gaius trembled with relief. One part of his plan had been fulfilled. Now for the other part.

"So you see," Gaius blurted out, speaking faster and faster as Adi stared at him. "You will be free, and Maria too. I know you hate being a slave. But freedom with no money has no future here in Rome. It was the best solution I could think of."

Adi steepled her fingers in front of her nose. "You want me to marry you." The shiver she felt had nothing to do with the autumn breeze that knocked more leaves from the lemon trees.

"Yes."

There were so many things wrong with this proposal. She didn't love him but how many marriages had love? He was kind. He was a Roman, though—she hated Romans… but at Masada she had been betrothed to a Jew who had been violent and cruel. She would be free. But would she be chained to this man?

Gaius must have sensed her hesitation. "If it doesn't work out, we can divorce. But at least you'll have a chance. I'll make sure we don't starve. I respect you, Adi. Many marriages are built on less."

She looked up at the cloudless sky. The breeze lifted again, rustling her skirts. She inhaled and stood, taking Gaius' hands. He was warm. "I will." The breeze dropped and the moment lingered. The stars shone and her hands tingled as she realised she trusted this man. They had friendship, maybe even affection. The rest might grow.

I chose to live. Now I choose to make a life.

Adi looked in Gaius' eyes. He leant in slowly and brushed his lips against hers. Her breath caught. "I will be a good husband to you," he promised.

"I know," she whispered as butterflies danced in her stomach. She lifted her mouth to his and let her fears slide away. He wrapped an arm around her waist and pulled her close. Heat swamped her as his lips caressed hers, drifting down her face and neck until he stopped with a shuddering breath.

"You'd best go in." He stepped back a fraction and brought her fingers to his lips. Adi nodded, exhilarated but relieved. The passion she felt from him was unlike anything she'd experienced. She'd seen desire in men's eyes for her body, but Gaius offered more.

"Until tomorrow," she smiled shyly and tugged her hands free.

Gaius returned the smile and leant down for one last, swift kiss. "Tomorrow."

Adi's heart sang as she crawled onto her pallet that night. *Freedom.* She rolled over and smiled in the dark. *Freedom... and maybe even love.*

Perhaps the road that led her to Rome had been worth it.

A SOLDIER'S LOVE

"She is dead, my lord." Meric bowed to Prince Stephen of Moldavia, burying his sadness in formality.

If the Prince felt any grief at the death of his sister, he didn't show it. Meric supposed he couldn't—after all, the rest of the world thought Alina had perished twelve years ago, throwing herself from the ramparts of a castle rather than be captured by the Ottomans.

"Thank you, Captain," Stephen beckoned Meric up. "And the convent?"

Meric supposed this was the Prince's way of asking if Alina had died in comfort. "It prospers, my lord. They were able to procure poppy-juice for Sister Mary before she passed, to ease her pain." It had been small comfort to Meric—on her deathbed, Alina had been gaunt, features ravaged by disease. Women didn't attract him, but Meric mourned the loss of Alina's beauty.

"Very good." Stephen nodded. "Now, you recall my cousin, Prince Vlad."

The change in topic would have seemed jarring to an outsider, but the connection was clear to Meric. Now that Vlad's wife, Alina, was truly dead, it left Vlad free to remarry. *Not that bigamy is the worst sin on his black soul.*

"Er, still a guest of King Matthias Corvinus." Twelve years as a prisoner of the Hungarian king wasn't enough, in his opinion, but he knew Stephen manoeuvred to have Vlad freed. The Prince needed a strong ally against the Ottomans, whose grasp and influence crept farther and farther into Europe as the years went by.

The Prince grunted amusement. "A guest, indeed." He pulled a letter from his surcoat and handed it to Meric. It was tightly furled and sealed with Stephen's signet. "Captain, you shall deliver this to Prince Vlad at the Fortress of Visegrad. I have already arranged with King Corvinus for you to escort my cousin back to Pest where he shall marry Princess Justina. You are to remain with him as part of his household guard along with the others that go with you." Stephen stood and strode to the tapestry that hung on his right. It showed a woven map of Moldavia, Wallachia and Transylvania, with the Ottoman Empire and the Kingdom of Hungary gnawing from opposite sides. "I will see you again in the spring when we go to war."

A sense of dread hung over Meric as he exited the dining hall, the letter packed safely into a leather satchel. His heavy footsteps took him to the stables where his horse was already saddled and waiting. Five other Moldavian soldiers waited there; he recognised Petro, Angelo, Christof and Boris. The fifth soldier was new—a stocky, dark-haired young man with an easy smile. He caught Meric's eye and nudged Petro. "The Captain's here, sir—we ready to go?"

"Mount up!" Petro barked. He was Meric's right-hand man, a scarred veteran of many campaigns against the Turks.

Meric swung into his saddle and gave the order to ride out. There would be time enough to worry about how he would face Vlad, let alone how he would serve him.

Despite the hard pace they set, being on the road gave Meric satisfaction. The hills were vibrant with summer life—farmers harvested crops and worked in leafy orchards. It was easy to buy food and pleasant to sleep under the stars each night. The new soldier, Mikhail, was given all the muckiest chores but he maintained a cheery air. Meric approved. Doing as you were told, and putting up with the occasional teasing was the fastest way to earn acceptance in a squad. Part of him remembered the unchecked bullying that had come in the barracks of the janissaries. Only favour from Prince Mehmed or his lovers protected a small boy from constant heckling. *All soldiers are like that, though. You toughen up, find favour or you suffer.* He knew it could go too far, so he quietly signalled approval of Mikhail and the men eased up.

As they climbed the foothills of the Carpathians, Meric's thoughts darkened.

"So is Dracula as ghastly as they say?" Mikhail asked one evening as they sat around the campfire. Angelo and Christof were on watch, the rest munched on roast rabbit.

"Ask the Captain," Petro grunted. "He's met him." He returned to his food.

Mikhail turned wide eyes to Meric. "Is it true he butchered a whole town of Saxons near Brașov?"

"Aye." Meric didn't want to elaborate.

"The Turks I can understand," Mikhail went on, "but Saxons? And I heard he marched to death hundreds of his own boyars, *and* their women and children."

Memories flooded into Meric. He stood and jabbed a rabbit bone in Mikhail's direction. "All you need to know is how to follow orders. Stop gossiping and practise your swordplay if you need something to do." He stomped away, looking for a tree to piss on. *Why did you lose your temper, you fool? You'll hear these damned tales over and over again before we reach Visegrad. Soldiers love a good horror story, and these men are about to meet one.*

He laced up his fly and strode away from the campsite, nodding to Angelo as he passed. Up the hill he found a cluster of boulders and perched on the biggest one, brooding like an owl as the moonlight splashed across the trees below. He could smell the woodsmoke from the fire, as well as the fresh air rolling off the mountains, and the musk of some large animal—a bear most likely—that had rubbed against the rocks.

A scuffling footstep made him slide off the boulder and draw his sword in one swift movement. With the rock between him and his potential attacker, he readied himself for a fight.

"Captain?"

Meric straightened. "Mikhail? You idiot, what are you doing up here? I could have killed you!" He rounded the boulder to see a dark figure standing there. He could smell Mikhail too—not an unpleasant scent like the bear spoor, simply the smell of male sweat, leather and horse.

"I wasn't sure which way you'd come," Mikhail said. "Should I not have spoken about Dracula?"

Huh? Any other soldier Meric had ever reprimanded had either shut up and fallen in line, or behaved mutinously until a physical confrontation blew up. No one had ever come to talk privately. He noticed Mikhail didn't blame Petro, either.

"Never mind it," Meric grunted.

Mikhail stepped closer. Meric could see his face in the moonlight, dark eyes fathomless, but the tone was clear. "Is he really so terrible?" The light curiosity held an undernote of fear.

Meric remembered hiding in the latrines all those years ago while Vlad and his men went on a killing rampage. He thought of thirty thousand Turks, impaled and left to rot in the summer sun as a warning to the Sultan not to advance any further. No wonder Gwyn had been terrified of the man who'd tried to rape her multiple times. Now he was being ordered by Prince Stephen to serve the monster, and he didn't know if he could do it.

"He is," he said gruffly. "But Prince Stephen gave us orders." Maybe they would be lucky. Maybe they would arrive in Hungary to find Vlad had perished from disease or accident. Prince Stephen would be furious—years of political machinations wrought for nothing—but there was always another war to fight, and Meric would fight it. That's what soldiers did.

Mikhail stood silently, then reached a hand and gripped Meric's shoulder briefly. "Orders are orders, Captain."

A shock ran through Meric at the other man's touch. A hot flush swept over him as he said gruffly, "Get back to camp. You're on next watch." He turned away and waited until he sensed the other man leave, then stood for a long time.

The tension continued—now that Meric was aware of it, he realised it had always been there. Mikhail's dark eyes and easy smile sent a ripple of excitement through him in a way he'd repressed for so many years. This wasn't the court at Constantinople, where the Prince took male lovers and passion between soldiers was quietly tolerated. He knew it happened—men like him were acutely aware of the tiny signals from other men who shared the same preferences—but the risk was enormous and the consequences for being found out were fatal.

He stomped into camp one evening after checking the horses. "Mikhail! You're on watch with Christof! Look lively! If a bandit falls out of the tree on you are you going to snore at him?"

Mikhail leapt up from where he'd been sitting at the fire, staring dreamily into the flames. He glanced at the moon in the sky—it was barely above the trees, he and Christof wouldn't be relieving Petro and Boris for a while yet. "Sorry, Captain!" He glanced at Christof, who grinned and kept eating.

"Hmph." Meric raked his gaze over the young soldier. "Finish your meal and clean up." He was glad that his gruff attitude wasn't emulated by the other men, who ironically seemed to have had their fill of hazing.

A week later they crossed the northern reaches of the Transylvanian Plateau. Villages and farms were scarce and they were forced to spend more time hunting. Shortly after dawn one morning, Christof and Boris stayed with the horses while Petro and Angelo set snares. Meric took Mikhail armed with crossbows and spears as they searched for bigger game. They moved quietly through the woods, bagging two wild geese. Meric was as conscious of the other man's movements as he was of the sounds and scents of the surrounding forest.

The trees grew thicker. Despite the bright sun overhead, the shade under the thick boughs was cool and smelled of moss. A scuffling in the bushes prompted both men to freeze. Something grunted. Meric's hand was on his crossbow—he reached for a bolt.

The breeze shifted. The grunt turned into a furious snort as a boar charged out of the bushes. Meric dropped the crossbow and grabbed his spear. "Here!" he shouted, drawing the animal's attention.

It moved faster than he expected, dodging his spear nimbly and almost goring him, but he leapt backwards in time. He swung the spear and gashed the boar's side. It grunted and charged again.

Mikhail dove across his field of vision and tackled the boar, stabbing wildly with his dagger. The animal squealed and bucked but Mikhail held on. He struck the beast in the eye and it emitted a last, desperate wheeze. It collapsed, twitching.

Meric drove his spear through the boar's neck just to be sure, then hauled Mikhail up by a blood-soaked arm. "You damned fool! You don't go after a boar with a fucking knife!"

Mikhail gasped, shock bright in his eyes. Meric grasped his shoulders and patted frantically down arms and chest. "Are you hurt?" he demanded.

Mikhail heaved a breath. "No. I'm fine. I just saw him charge you and couldn't load my crossbow in time!"

Overwhelmed, Meric hugged the other man tightly then thumped Mikhail on the chest. "Where was your fucking spear?" He hugged him again then pulled back, aware that his fright was making him careless.

Mikhail gave a small smile. "Were you worried, Captain?" The look in his eyes caught Meric's breath.

Meric snapped the lid shut on his emotions. "You're covered in blood. Help me truss up the damned animal and we'll head back to camp. There's a stream half a mile back—you can clean up there." He turned away and yanked his spear from the dead boar.

They worked in silence, gutting and tying hooves together. Laden with the boar, the two geese from earlier, and their weapons, they tramped back through the forest, stopping at the stream. Meric looked at the sun—it was only noon. They weren't expected back at the camp before nightfall. "Clean yourself up," he ordered.

Meric stripped his leather jerkin off and dragged his shirt over his head. Crouching by the stream, he soaked the linen in the cool water and sponged himself with the wet fabric. He sighed, feeling back in control.

That feeling vanished as he stood and glanced at Mikhail. The other man had also taken off his shirt to wash. Water dripped down a muscular chest, but the look in Mikhail's eyes was anything but cool. Meric knew he should look away, but held his gaze as Mikhail stepped closer. Meric's breath came short and he opened his mouth to say something—what, he didn't know.

"No." Mikhail raised a finger to Meric's lips, placing the other hand on his chest. As if in a dream, Meric gripped both of Mikhail's hands, kissing both palms. Mikhail closed his eyes, lips parted. Meric kissed those lips next and was rewarded with a small groan of desire. They sank to their knees by the stream; the boar and their stained shirts forgotten.

"Did I hurt you," Meric asked sometime later, as they re-washed their shirts and wrung them out by the stream. He was rewarded again with that small smile.

"Only at first," Mikhail answered, gazing shyly at Meric. His brief confidence seemed to have evaporated but Meric could feel the passion emanate between them still.

Meric stroked Mikhail's cheek, then strode to their gear, his thoughts churning. Making love to Mikhail had stoked a roaring fire of want in him. But what if no opportunity to be alone together arose? Or worse, what if they did manage to be alone together and Mikhail pretended nothing had happened? *How will I survive the rest of this journey, let alone service to Vlad the Butcher, if I can't be with him?*

He turned abruptly. "We should get back to camp."

The next few days were hard, and that included the feeling in Meric's breeches every time he thought about Mikhail for too long. He tried to behave exactly the same, though he was aware he became moodier and snappier as they crossed the Hungarian border. He didn't dare change the watch rotation, so it wasn't until they neared the twin cities of Buda and Pest that his turn fell with Mikhail again. After being woken by Christof and Petro, they silently made their way into the woods, separated to complete a circuit of the camp, then re-met to fall upon each other with mutual, desperate abandon. Mouths met as they tugged at belts and shirts. Meric was conscious of the rest of his men sleeping two dozen yards away. Mikhail tugged Meric's breeches down, trailing kisses as he went. Meric clutched Mikhail's shoulder, trying to keep silent, but in the end couldn't stop the moan that escaped him. Mikhail gently pushed Meric to the ground and pulled his own breeches down. Fingers entwined and Meric was overwhelmed by the rush of heat that engulfed him again.

Then a twig snapped and they both froze.

"Just a fox," murmured Mikhail and resumed his slow, deliberate rhythm.

Meric prayed he was right, because nothing was stopping Mikhail now.

Later, Meric kissed Mikhail's neck as they lay together on a carpet of autumn leaves. "This is dangerous," he murmured.

Mikhail chuckled. "I know." He twisted to face Meric and kissed his mouth. "But worth it."

A wolf howled in the distance. In the trees above them, an owl hooted. Meric breathed in Mikhail's scent, reluctant to tear himself away from the other man's warmth. "Why me?" he asked.

Mikhail stroked Meric's face. "Why you, Captain? Does there need to be a reason? You're strong yet fair. You care for the men you lead. I knew this about you even before I was assigned to your squad."

"I wasn't fair to you before."

Mikhail shrugged. "You have an instinct for self-preservation. Isn't that what makes a good soldier?"

"Why did you become a soldier?"

A snort of derision. "It was either that or marry the crofter's daughter and be a farmer in the pig-shit village I grew up in. What would you choose?"

Meric sat up and fumbled for his shirt. He pulled it on. "I never had a choice."

Mikhail grabbed Meric's hand. When Mikhail didn't say anything, Meric let himself be stilled. "Come now," he sighed. "Let's stand watch."

They reached Buda and were escorted to the palace high on the hill above the Danube, overlooking the sister city of Pest on the opposite bank. Once inside the palace, a chamberlain of King Matthias Corvinus received Meric.

"You will not have to go to Visegrad," he informed Meric brusquely. "The king has ordered an official Hungarian escort to bring back his new, beloved brother-in-law as a token of his esteem."

Meric's black mood lifted in a heartbeat. Duty dictated that he state, "I have a letter from Prince Stephen of Moldavia for Prince Vlad."

"I will include it with the official letter from the king—you can be sure it will not go astray."

Meric couldn't argue with that—to do so would have been an insult. Besides, the prospect of another week or so with Mikhail in a city where private rooms and bathhouses were easy to find was much more appealing than traipsing upriver to the grim fortress of Visegrad to retrieve a man he hated.

"Good news, lads!" he announced as he returned to the tavern where they had found lodgings. He pulled the door shut against the chill autumn wind. "We get to wait here for the Prince to return from his country stay. King Matthias is sending his own men to fetch him."

A cheer met his words, except for Petro who didn't raise his mug of ale. The others continued drinking—Mikhail's faced glowed with quiet happiness in the firelight.

"Bit of an insult to Prince Stephen, not trusting us to collect Dracula." Petro frowned at Meric, who signalled for ale.

Meric shrugged and sat. "Bigger insult to King Matthias to say that, and I know who's near and who's far." The barmaid placed his ale down and smiled at him. Meric smiled absently in return, then turned a more genuine grin at Mikhail.

Petro's frown deepened. "Trust a mercenary to say that," he muttered.

Meric's smile snapped to a stern look. "Got something to say, Petro?"

Petro returned his stare mulishly. "No, Captain."

What's brought this on? Meric had never had a problem with Petro before—the man had always been solid and reliable, if taciturn.

The rest of the evening continued without remark—effectively released from duty the men joyfully discovered the famous bathhouses of Buda and Pest, many of them adjoining upmarket brothels. Meric didn't get drunk—his upbringing in the Empire restrained him. Mikhail was not so cautious. Meric had to hustle him from a bathhouse one evening under the guise of looking for a whore before Mikhail's affection became too obvious.

"Damn you," Meric muttered, pulling Mikhail into a dark alley and kissed him fiercely as the rain pattered onto their oiled leather cloaks. "Do you want everyone to see?"

"I hate having to hide," Mikhail whispered and chuckled. "I wish I could kiss you in front of them all and see their faces."

Meric reached down and grasped his lover's crotch, causing Mikhail to gasp and grind against him. "It's a death sentence. You've got me acting like a damned fool. I want you up against this wall this minute."

Mikhail reached down and grabbed Meric's wrist, stilling him. His eyes gazed soulfully at Meric. "Is that all you want from me, Captain? My arse?"

No. The feeling that had been growing in Meric for the past few weeks threatened to burst his heart. His need to be close to Mikhail was surpassed by a longing that had been unfulfilled these past twelve years. Meric's first love, Vlad's brother Radu, had forgotten him. He'd resigned himself to the occasional, furtive liaison, thinking he could never have the kind of love that he truly wanted.

Then Mikhail had shattered all that, and hope bloomed in his heart.

"No." He straightened and lifted his hand to Mikhail's face. "I want all of you. I need you. Let us find somewhere to be alone."

A messenger came from the palace after five days. They were to meet Vlad at the northern gate of Pest, whereupon his Hungarian escort would officially hand him over to the Moldavians and they would (in the messenger's words) 'ride triumphantly to Prince Vlad's new official residence and meet his royal bride, Princess Justina.' Meric spared a moment of pity for the princess, but reserved most of his gloom for himself. How would he and Mikhail continue with the spectre of Vlad looming over them? They might be executed or exiled if discovered under normal circumstances, but if Vlad found out he was likely to impale or dismember them while still alive.

Petro, on the other hand, was brighter and more cheerful than Meric had ever seen him. "Dracula fought the Turks tooth and nail," Petro told Christof, Boris and Angelo. "He slaughtered thousands in the name of Christendom. With him at Prince Stephen's side they'll drive those Moselmen back into the sea." Petro caught Meric's eye as he spoke and scratched his neck idly. Meric's hand itched, wanting to touch the crescent-moon tattoo on his own neck, a remnant of his upbringing in the Empire. Petro knew Meric wasn't a native-Moldavian. But in the years they'd served Prince Stephen together it had never been an issue. Why was it now?

Meric's stomach twisted. Did Petro suspect something? It wouldn't be the first time discovery of two men as lovers caused an extreme, irrational reaction. He touched his scarred half-ear. What if Petro was waiting until Vlad arrived, and sought advancement by way of Meric's demise?

What should he do?

"What's wrong?" Mikhail whispered in his ear that night, having snuck into Meric's room at the tavern through the outer window.

"Nothing." It was a lie. Everything was wrong. He thought he'd escaped Vlad. Now duty would chain him to the man.

"Meric."

Meric twisted to look at his lover. It was the first time Mikhail had used his name. "We have to flee. We'll go west, to the Germanies. Or Italy—I've heard mercenaries do well there."

Mikhail shook his head and smiled. "I'm not afraid, Meric. We'll be careful."

"I don't doubt your courage, my love, but Vlad is… he is to be feared no matter how brave you are." He wished Gwyn was here, that she could spirit Mikhail and him away with her magic amulet.

Mikhail kissed him. "Prince Stephen sent us to serve Prince Vlad. It is our duty."

If I argue, he will think me a coward, or a faithless man with no loyalty to his Prince. He doesn't know that I am faithless, that I fought against the land of my childhood, and then against the land of my faith. He deserves better than me.

His head told him to flee, but his heart beckoned. He would stay, and try to be worthy of Mikhail.

Trumpets blared. Horses whinnied and the crowd around the gate cheered. *They wouldn't cheer if they knew what kind of a man he was.* Meric forced himself to ease his grip on the reins. Vlad Dracula rode into sight, heading a small procession of Hungarian royal soldiers. As they neared, Meric shouted, "Salute!" His men stood in their stirrups, raised sword and spear and clashed them together, then sat at attention in their saddles. Meric could be proud of them at least. Every weapon, buckle and stirrup gleamed; the horses were groomed beautifully, and Vlad's own standard flew above Prince Stephen's from the pole Angelo carried.

Vlad trotted through the gate and Meric signalled his men to fall in, with Angelo riding ahead. The Hungarian soldiers dropped back until the changeover had taken place. They rode through the streets of Pest until they reached the grand mansion the king had allocated Vlad. At no point did Vlad acknowledge any of his escort, Hungarian or Moldavian. When they reached the mansion's front gate he rode straight through and dismounted at the huge oak front door. He pulled off his gloves and tossed them at the servant who held the door open. Meric kept his face impassive as he dismounted and followed, waving a hand at the others to dismiss them.

Vlad continued past the entrance hall into the dining room—a large chamber richly furnished but with an air of age. The tapestries were worn at the edges, the oak table had scratches. "Wine!" he barked. The servant hastened to obey, pouring from a ready flagon into a silver goblet that Vlad snatched and downed as he sat at the head of the table.

Meric hesitated just inside the door, eyeing his new master. Never tall, Vlad's muscular form had thickened, and grey threaded its way through his mass of dark curls, but the sense of menace he exuded was still present. Here was a man who liked to kill, and was good at it. More than that, he relished causing pain.

Vlad looked at Meric. Flickers of emotions showed in his eyes—surprise, rage, calculation. "You," Vlad spat, setting his goblet down with a thud.

"My lord." Meric bowed, hating the submission he was obligated to show.

Vlad drummed his fingers on the table, then gestured to the servant. "More wine! Then leave us. Shut the door behind you." He waited until they were alone then rose, stalking towards Meric. Vlad halted and looked Meric over, hatred in his eyes. "Why are you here?"

Meric controlled his voice. "Prince Stephen sent me to command your household guard."

Vlad sneered. "Does my dear cousin know he harbours a traitorous sodomite in his midst? Obviously not, or he would have hanged you and had your entrails staked out for the crows."

"Prince Stephen knows I was once a janissary, my lord, that I was part of the same tribute that took you when we were children. He also knows I have served him faithfully these past twelve years, fighting against the Turks and…" Mentioning Alina was a bad idea, so he said instead, "and being a trusted member of his royal guard."

"Hmph."

Tension coiled between them. Meric desperately wanted to draw his sword and hack the man down where he stood. But he'd overcome that urge before, for the sake of someone he cared about. He would do so again.

Vlad snorted and stalked back to his wine, reseating himself. "Very well. Next week I marry Princess Justina. Tomorrow I am to attend on King Matthias and begin planning the war against the imposter who sits on my throne. Every other day I want to go hunting, now that I'm out of that damn shithole they call Visegard. See to it."

He flicked his fingers in dismissal. Meric thanked the years of training as a soldier that he automatically bowed and answered, "Yes, my lord." Hesitation could be fatal. He had drummed into his men to show Vlad the utmost respect at all times, but he would reinforce the lesson.

Especially to Mikhail.

Meric and his men served Vlad tirelessly in weeks that followed. Hunting trips, formal visits to the palace, even the wedding to Princess Justina passed without incident. The household grew with the addition of the princess' extensive entourage of servants and ladies, whilst the steward took care of Vlad's day-to-day habits. Meric was left to organise guard rosters, training, and other duties, which suited him. The less he had to do with Vlad, the better.

Then came the night of the thief.

The first Meric knew of the disturbance was shouting and the thud of the front door. He leapt up from his pallet and buckled his sword belt, shoving feet into boots and leaving nightshirt trailing as he burst from his small room adjoining the guardhouse. "What's going on?" he demanded of Mikhail, who had been on duty. "Where's Boris?"

"A thief!" Mikhail shouted excitedly. "He climbed over the wall because the Watch were chasing him! We let them in to help capture him. Boris went into the house while I stayed on guard."

Meric assessed the situation. Mikhail had closed the gate but guarding alone wasn't ideal. "Petro! Angelo! Christof!"

Petro had already tumbled out of bed. "What's happening, Captain?"

"Guard the gate. I'm going to find out what's going on inside." As Angelo and Christof appeared, nightshirts hastily stuffed into breeches, Meric added, "Mikhail, come with me. I need an eyewitness. The rest of you, make sure no one else enters or leaves."

He strode towards the open front door, sword in hand. Mikhail ran to catch up. *Please let Vlad be in a deep slumber, or too busy swiving his new wife to hear.*

They entered the house. The thief lay semi-conscious, on the floor, a triumphant Hungarian watchman standing over him. The watchman kicked the thief in the stomach and turned to his companions. "Good work, lads! Thanks for your help, my friend," he said to Boris in bad Romanian, who grinned.

"Saw the little bastard slinking over the wall. You picked the wrong house, you festering turd."

"He certainly did." Vlad's voice floated down from the grand staircase that led to the uppers levels.

Dread pitted in Meric's stomach. They all turned to look at the Prince, still dressed as he had been for dinner in a red velvet surcoat over black robes. Vlad toyed with a long dagger, tapping the blade in his palm as he walked down the stairs.

"Forgive the intrusion, my lord," the captain of the watchmen bobbed his head in a quick bow. He spoke Hungarian, of which Meric understood enough. "This thief fled the scene of his crime and we chased him here. We'll be on our way and see he gets the justice he deserves. Sorry about the disturbance." He gestured to his men and turned his back.

To Meric, it was as though the world had slowed to the speed of cold treacle. He watched Vlad leave the bottom step and heard him say in perfect Hungarian, "A moment, Watchman." The Watch captain turned enquiringly and Vlad's hand flashed out, burying the dagger in the captain's throat. The thief screamed as blood sprayed across him. Shouts of dismay and protest from the other guards sounded far away and Meric found himself unable to move as Vlad roared, "I am a *prince*! How dare you enter my house without permission? How *dare* you disrespect me!"

Time sped up and Meric looked down at the blood on his nightshirt. He looked back at the Hungarian watchmen, who were white with terror.

"GET OUT!" Vlad bellowed.

They scrambled to flee. One grabbed the fallen captain while the other dragged the whimpering thief behind him. A smear of blood chased them along the floor and outside.

"Shut that door," Vlad said in a normal voice. "It's chilly out there."

Meric walked over and shut it. He returned to where Vlad waited, wondering what would happen next.

"Who permitted those guards into my house?" The tone that had boiled with fury a moment ago now could have frosted glass.

"Er." Meric needed to protect his men. "I did, my lord."

Vlad looked Meric up and down, taking in the trailing nightshirt, the unlaced boots and the lopsided sword belt. "No, you did not, Captain."

"I did, my lord." Mikhail stood to attention and bowed. "I was on duty and knew we could not catch the thief without assistance and still guard the gate. Boris helped them catch the man, but I opened the gate to them."

Shut up, you damned fool! Meric was aghast. *Did you not see what he just did?*

"Is this how you train your men, Captain?" Vlad breathed, stepping close to Meric. "To let armed foreigners in, foreigners that disrespect my name and my station. How can I trust soldiers such as this? Will they let the Turks in while I sleep, to slit my throat and rape my wife? What other deviant habits have you taught them?"

Meric could see how this would go. Even if Vlad didn't lash out at this instant it was only a matter of time. He would relish Meric's fear even before he inflicted any physical pain upon him. He would torture Mikhail and Boris for their error; publicly, privately, he wouldn't care.

What is my duty?

"If you need to make an example of me, my lord, I suggest you do it in front of all of my men." A risky move, but one that would buy him time. He quashed his fear and stared Vlad in the eyes.

Vlad's moustache quirked. "A fair point, Captain." He yawned. "Clean up this damned mess, I'm going to bed." He spun on his heel and strode up the stairs, disappearing into his private chambers.

Silence reigned. "Is he mad?" whispered Boris.

Meric felt old. "No. He's always been like this." He made a decision. "Boris, go and tell the others what happened. Mikhail, find a servant to mop up this blood and meet me back at the guardhouse." He left them and went straight to his room, lit a candle, dressed properly, and started packing his things.

Mikhail found him. "What are you doing?"

Meric looked at Mikhail. "I cannot serve one such as him. He is cruel, he kills for sport. There is nothing noble about him. And he will kill you if he finds out I care for you, just to hurt me. He's always wanted to hurt me."

"You intend to leave." There was no accusation, just bland statement.

Meric slumped. "I can't protect you here. I won't even be able to protect myself." He hated the weakness he heard in his voice. Hated that he couldn't meet Mikhail's eye. He continued to shove spare clothes, a set of knives, and various accoutrements, into his saddlebags.

Mikhail's footsteps receded. Meric's heart cracked but he shoved the feeling down, buckled his saddlebags and swung them over his shoulder. He tried to get his head straight—he needed a good lie to get past his men at the gate. At the stables he lit a torch and readied his horse. He stopped when the door opened behind him. Meric turned.

Mikhail stood there, his own packs in hand. "I told Petro and the others that the Prince was sending you and me to the Palace to complain about the invasion of his property. If we're quick they won't notice we're laden for a journey."

Meric swallowed. "Mikhail." His voice came out gruff.

Mikhail smiled. "Where you go, I go, Captain."

A SOLDIER'S HONOUR

If it hadn't been for the whore in the marketplace, Meric and Mikhail never would have found work. Mercenaries were viewed suspiciously by the good burgers of Regensburg, and for good reason. Mercenaries who blew in from the east, reeking of Slavic customs and Ottoman influences, were judged even more harshly than the usual good-for-naught-but-killing, hard-faced soldiers of fortune who clustered in bars and brothels, seeking war and work.

Fleeing Hungary and the wrath of Prince Vlad Dracula, Meric and Mikhail had journeyed to the Germanies. Regensburg had a reputation for mercenary recruitment.

"Let's try another tavern," Meric suggested when an afternoon's drinking had proved fruitless. They crossed the marketplace, looking for another drinking den. Mikhail stopped and inhaled, taking in the scent of roasted chestnuts and spiced pastries from a nearby food cart. The light was failing as dark clouds rolled in and the air sizzled with static. Several stallholders persisted despite the imminent storm, shouting end-of-day clearance prices as they hastened to shift their wares.

"You lads look far from home," a woman's voice broke through Mikhail's reverie. He didn't want to keep drinking—he wanted a bowl of stew and a private room where he could worship his lover's body—but they needed to find work, and for soldiers that meant drinking.

"Not far enough!" Meric joked.

The brunette sauntered over from the mouth of the alley where she had been loitering, swaying her hips and smiling. "Near or far, you could use a bit o' comfort, I'm sure. Do you a good price for the both of you?" Now that she was close, Mikhail could see how thin she was, despite the way she thrust her bosom forwards in her low cut dress. Her nose was crooked, like it had been broken in the past, but she couldn't have been any older than him. Whores aged badly.

"Aye, mistress, but we're short on coin," Meric replied apologetically. "You don't want to waste your time with us; we seek a company to take us on. Perhaps then we'll seek your wares."

The whore's smile fell. "Well, sod off and bugger each other, then. I won't get no customers with you crowding my patch."

Mikhail would have angrily replied that she was the one who had approached them, but choked in panic instead at her first sentence. The whore eyed him sharply.

Meric boomed a laugh. "You've upset my friend, mistress." He punched Mikhail—a little too hard—in the shoulder, warning him.

The whore's eyes slid from one man to the other, and Mikhail came to his senses enough to grind out, "The insult… to my honour."

The whore rolled her eyes. "Oh, to be a man, and have the luxury of honour. You boys just seeking a billet then? I work the streets, don't take no customers home. Can rent you the room, cheap like?"

Mikhail exchanged glances with Meric. A billow of cold air flooded his nostrils as he inhaled. It would rain soon. "I don't think we're going to have any luck tonight, captain." Meric was captain no longer, but Mikhail used the rank rather than speak Meric's name and give away his obvious affection.

"Aye." Meric sighed. "Are your lodgings far, mistress? Where will you sleep?"

"I'll bunk in with a friend." Businesslike, the whore snapped her narrow shoulders around and led the way from the market, off the cobbled streets and through a dirty alley. They passed scavenging dogs and climbed a rickety wooden staircase. She unlocked the door with a key hung from a string around her neck, and gestured for them to enter the dark, poky room. "I don't keep no money here, so there's naught to steal."

"How much?" Meric asked. She named a price that was outrageously high. He countered with a figure a quarter of that. She came back with a half, and they settled on a third. Meric handed over the coin in exchange for the key.

"Mistress Braun on the corner does hot meals. Tell her Heidi sent you. You can leave the key with her in the morning if I ain't back." The whore, Heidi, vanished the payment into her skirts and nodded. "I'd best get back to it. There's coin to be made before the weather turns nasty."

After she left, Meric turned to Mikhail. "Something to eat before it pisses down?"

Bellies full, the thunder chased them back to the room where Mikhail lit a solitary candle and then opened the shutters to air the room and watch the pattering rain drift over rooftops amidst flashes of lightning. Meric circled his arms around him, kissing Mikhail's neck. "Nice to be out of it," he murmured, "even if it is a shitty dive."

Mikhail hummed contentedly. "It's a palace to me. It's got you, me, and no one else." They'd slept rough for weeks, braving the early winter weather. What shelter they'd paid for had been cheap, common rooms with assorted pallets and little privacy.

Meric sighed. "You lost a lot because of me."

Mikhail turned, still encircled, angry. "I would've lost a lot more serving that bastard of a prince. I chose you. I love you."

Meric silenced him, covering his mouth with warmth, tenderness and—as the kiss deepened—desire. Mikhail responded in kind, reaching up to cup Meric's rough-whiskered face, sliding his hand round the taller man's neck, drawing him close.

The time without privacy showed. Mikhail chafed at having to hide his feelings. Since finding Meric, he wanted to spend every moment pressed up against him, and to hell with the risk. He loved to find ways to tempt Meric, overcoming the older man's caution but secretly grateful that one of them was level headed enough to keep them both alive. All the hardships in the world—the cold, the lack of money and food—were tolerable with Meric at his side.

Mikhail felt himself grow hard and he ground himself against his lover. He felt Meric grin, felt his hand slide down to Mikhail's waist to cup his arse. "I'm gonna take my time with you tonight," Meric whispered, his breath hot in Mikhail's ear.

"Stuff that," Mikhail responded. "I want you now."

Meric chuckled and kissed him again, pushing the younger man's jacket off his shoulders and drawing his shirt from his breeches. "So impatient, soldier." He teased kisses down Mikhail's neck, causing Mikhail to clench his fists and fumble at Meric's clothes. "Uh uh," Meric admonished with a devious smile, pushing him back to sit on the narrow bed. Mikhail ripped his shirt off and sat impatiently, twitching with want as Meric shed his own layers, as serene as if he was undressing for a bath. The only tell was the intensity in his eyes, filled with such affection and desire that Mikhail swallowed hard, wondering what he'd done to deserve the love of this incredible man.Who leaned forward and kissed him slowly.

Mikhail groaned softly. "You're a right bastard. Hurry up and take your pants off."

Meric straightened. His boots, stockings and breeches followed the shirt and jacket. Mikhail fought the urge to leap off the bed and do him on the floor, cold and dirty though it was. Meric clearly sensed the impatience and grinned again but took pity, divesting Mikhail of the rest of his clothes until he knelt naked and was worshiping the younger man with his mouth. Mikhail moaned, eyes rolled back as he gripped Meric's russet-brown hair. "You bastard," he breathed, "I, uh, you bastard."

"Mmm," Meric hummed, sending Mikhail into a hip-jolting frenzy. It didn't take long at all, for which he was both sorry and grateful, but it meant Meric's comforting warmth was soon embracing his entire body as he lay back on the bed.

"What?" Mikhail asked lazily. "That's it?"

"Oh no." Meric's voice was deep and rough. "I've got you right where I want you now." His hand traced downwards, exploring into places that had Mikhail moan again. Their joining was tantalisingly slow. Despite his earlier release Mikhail still wanted Meric, wanted him with his whole body and soul. They kissed with fierce abandon, Meric breathing harder and harder until he lost control, shuddering into completion, his face pressed into Mikhail's neck.

"You're mine," Mikhail whispered, feeling joy that he was the only one who saw this side of his captain. "No one else's."

"Yours," Meric agreed, breathless.

They curled around each other, until Meric finally got up to close the shutters and blow out the candle. The rain beat harder outside, but in their warmth and bliss, Mikhail felt as secure and safe as his captain snored gently beside him, their troubles forgotten for a while.

Someone hammered on the door, jolting Mikhail awake and into irritation. "What in God's name...?" he muttered, rolling from the comforting embrace of Meric's warm chest and arms.

"Open up, Heidi, you slack bitch!" a man yelled, thumping the door again.

Mikhail heard the rustle of cloth and turned to catch the shirt Meric flung at him. Swiftly, both men dragged on shirts and laced breeches as the intruder continued to hammer and holler insults. Mikhail passed his lover his sword, and gripped the hilt of a long dagger himself before standing carefully beside the door and opening it with a jerk. A short, greasy-haired man stumbled forward, splattering rain from his sodden coat. "You'll pay for that you stupid slattern—who the hell are you? And you?" He caught sight of Meric, scabbarded sword in hand , and shrank into himself.

"Who are you?" Meric demanded.

Instead of answering, the weedy little man looked about shiftily. "Where's that slut, Heidi? She don't take customers home. And if she does she owes me my cut."

Mikhail drifted behind the man and pricked him in the arm with his knife. "My friend asked you a question." The man jumped and slapped a hand over the jab, glaring at Mikhail, who grinned dangerously. He caught Meric's slight frown.

"I'm Werner. Heidi's my whore. Where is she?"

"Not here," Meric replied shortly.

"What'd she charge you? She'd better not be keeping takings from me, or I'll break her bloody nose again!" Werner bobbed with indignation. Mikhail wanted to kick him in the kneecaps, make him show Meric the respect he deserved.

"We're not customers." Meric relaxed his grip on his sword, but drew himself up straighter. It always caught Mikhail's breath how imposing, how handsome his captain was, even in a half-tucked dirty shirt and patched breeches. Meric carried himself with an air of command and confidence, something he'd told Mikhail he'd learnt from a girl he'd once known. "Act like you're in charge, and people will believe it."

"Not customers?" Werner spat, disbelieving. He sniffed suspiciously, and a chill went down Mikhail's spine. Despite the air flooding in, the room smelled of sex, and there wasn't a woman in sight.

"We're cousins of Heidi's." Meric's voice brooked no argument. "She let us stay and went out to work. We don't know when she'll be back."

Werner licked his lips. "You tell that slut I'm looking for her, and she owes me my cut."

Mikhail gripped Werner's arms and spun him around to face the door. "Why don't you piss off while you've still got legs to walk on, friend. And don't go bothering our cousin. She'll find you when she's ready." He shoved the pimp outside and watched him skid down the first few rickety stairs before steadying himself on the rail. Drizzle pooled and beaded down Werner's face as he glared back up at Mikhail, but he said nothing and scurried away.

Mikhail shut the door with a clunk, then turned back to Meric. "What a whoreson."

Meric grunted, "Try not go stabbing everyone you meet, whoreson or no. I'd rather not get in too much trouble while we're here."

Mikhail sighed and put his knife down. He crossed to Meric, took the sword from his hand and knelt to lay it on the floor with a clunk. Staying on his knees, he tugged the laces of Meric's breeches and dragged them down. "How about we keep the stabbing to ourselves, then?"

Any answer of Meric's was drowned out by his groan of pleasure. As the rain beat heavier outside, they made the most of their private abode.

The rain finally abated mid-afternoon, and the two men ventured out to find food and scour the taverns again in search of soldiers who might introduce them to a mercenary captain seeking new recruits. They met with little success.

Fed and sated in other ways, Mikhail kept up a positive banter that had them chatting with men in various drinking dens. Meric had a quieter, but no less charismatic air that drew people to him, but all word was that any mercenary companies in town weren't hiring, they were just resting up for the winter.

They left the third tavern as evening fell, breath misting in the air before the wind whipped it away. As they approached yet another drinking den, an icy gust hit Mikhail in the face. A fist hit him harder from behind.

"Oi!" he heard Meric yell as he pitched forward, seeing stars. A blink, a roll and he was up again for the fight, seeing two thugs tackling Meric and another bruiser charging towards him.

Mikhail didn't waste time thinking. He ducked under the punch and sent a solid fist of his own into the guts of his attacker, hearing *oof* followed closely by a high-pitched groan as he kneed the balls of the man trying to take him down. He glanced up at Meric's grunt, seeing his lover step back with perfect timing and crash the skulls of the two thugs together. Dazed, they lurched back and Meric drew his sword with a swift movement, snarling, "Who wants a piece?"

Something stung and burned in his arm. He roared, hauling the knife-holding hand over his shoulder, sending the weedy pimp Werner crashing onto the slick cobbles. Furious the scumbag had got the jump on him, Mikhail kicked hard, and Werner's neck snapped sideways with a sickening crunch.

"Oh, shit." Meric's two attackers shoved through the growing crowd, fleeing the scene. Mikhail stared down at Werner's glassy eyes, his mouth askew. With a groan, the man Mikhail had kicked in the balls rolled to his feet and took off after the other thugs.

"Hold 'em, lads!" Another voice, a deep, authoritative one, commanded, and Mikhail found himself in the hard grip of two grim-faced soldiers. Across from him Meric was forced to drop his sword as a soldier twisted his arm. Meric grunted painfully, and Mikhail struggled.

"Take your hands off me!" he growled.

The deep-voiced man laughed, coming into view. The flickering torches bracketed on the outside of the tavern door cast a warm glow on his bearded face. "Bit of a scrap, lads? Oh dear, what do we 'ave 'ere?" He toed Werner's body, the corpse rapidly cooling on the freezing ground. "Spot o' murder."

"He attacked us!" Mikhail burst out.

"Mikhail!" Meric admonished. He faced the bearded man squarely. "We weren't looking for trouble."

"Seems you were," the bearded man said. "My lads said you've been asking around. You obviously know 'ow to 'andle yourselves, though this one looks like a bit of an 'ot'ead." He jabbed a thumb at Mikhail, who growled until Meric silenced him with a glare.

"I didn't mean to kill him, captain," Mikhail ground out. "He swiped me with his knife." The bright blood seeping between the fingers of one of the men holding him proved his words true, and Mikhail was silently grateful for the pressure on the wound. The reality of having murdered a man, even in self-defence, sank in. They were in a foreign town, with no friends and dozens of witnesses who had seen the fight. His stomach churned. They'd be strung up at the gallows without a moment's thought—troublesome vagrants disturbing the town's peace.

"… you're both military men," Beard was saying. "You fight with precision, not like those brawlers. You any good with that sword?" He nodded at Meric's blade, the metal glinting in the torchlight as it lay on the cobbles.

"Sword. Spear. Crossbow. Seen cannon in action too." Meric listed his qualifications matter-of-factly and Mikhail felt a glimmer of hope.

Beard peered at him with interest. "Cannon? And the 'othead 'ere calls you captain—you've led men."

"Aye." Meric held Beard's gaze.

Beard chuckled just as running feet and shouts were heard. Armoured men shoved through the crowd. Mikhail's heart sank and the sick feeling returned. It was the watch.

"Otto, what the fuck's going on here?" the watch sergeant demanded, rubbing his forehead and looking like he'd been dragged away from a cosy corner and a tankard of ale. His expression was that of someone who was distinctly unimpressed with the fact that murder had been committed in his town that night.

Otto, the bearded man, shrugged. "I was just 'aving a bite to eat when a brawl started up. Couple of local lads took offense to a few of mine. Not sure I appreciate it."

Confusion abounded in Mikhail brain, not helped by the lightheadedness that came from being suddenly released and his knife wound starting to bleed again. He staggered, and Meric, also freed, was across the space in an instant, holding him up.

"Anyone see the men who did this?" Otto boomed, and suddenly the crowd was very busy going in other directions, until only Otto's men, the watch, Meric and Mikhail stood in the chilly street. With one exception: a skinny prostitute hovered in the shadows. Determined to shake the label of hothead, Mikhail kept quiet, trying to work out what was going on.

The watch sergeant sighed. "God's balls, Otto, try to keep your bloody men in check. It's too bloody cold to run around on a night like this." As if his words were prophetic, several flakes of snow drifted into the flickering torchlight.

Otto clapped the sergeant on the shoulder. "Let me buy you an ale, and my lads will sort out this mess. Get that wound sorted out," he ordered Mikhail.

Flanked by Otto's men, Meric and Mikhail hobbled into the tavern and squeezed onto a bench near one of the fireplaces, displacing a grumbling moggy who had been purring by the hearth. The smell of roast meat wafted from the kitchen. Mikhail grit his teeth, feeling woozy from the sudden warmth. He'd be damned if he'd shame Meric in front of these men.

"Here, get that into ye." One of the soldiers shoved a tankard at Mikhail, and another at Meric. He grinned, showing broken teeth. "Welcome to the Black Ravens, lads."

"Aye!" cheered the men around him, unperturbed by the evening's events.

"What do we call you, killer?" A chunky soldier with several gold earrings sat back on his stool, scratching his belly.

Mikhail exchanged a look with Meric, who gave him a crooked smile. "Mikhail, and Meric." He caught sight of Heidi skulking in the corner—she had obviously slipped inside rather than shiver her wares in the cold. Mikhail raised his voice. "Best night's sleep I had last night thanks to you, wench!" he declared truthfully. She froze, like a deer in the hunter's sights, and glared at the sudden attention.

Meric followed Mikhail's gaze and nodded. "Well worth the extra rate!"

Distracted, and interested by this shining endorsement, the soldiers of the Black Ravens looked around. "What's your rate, lovely?" one man called.

Heidi gave Mikhail and his lover a curt nod, then offered a false smile to the soldier. "You got a room here?" She disappeared with him upstairs and Mikhail hoped the business meant she wouldn't starve this winter. He and Meric might be desperate, but it seemed like for now they would survive.

THE TIME-TRAVELLER'S DATE

2617 AD

Michelle straightened from her crouch as the blue haze dissipated and the Jump Room appeared around her. She cross-checked her arrival with the time display on the wall, mentally logged it in her chronokinetor, and popped the time-travel device from her hand.

"How'd I go?" she called up to the control room. The technician fist-bumped the glass with a grin. Michelle returned the smile, exhausted but elated. Getting a young Charles Darwin onto the Beagle had been the easy part. Checking in on him later in life had required subtlety, but as his publications made their way out into nineteenth century Earth she was confident of her success in repairing the timeline.

"Commissioner is on the com for you from Vivaldis." Another technician escorted Michelle from the Jump Room to Medic Bay. "Says you can report in while you get your post-mission checks."

As blood tests were taken and scans were done, a hologram flickered into view above the computer nearby.

"Congratulations, Agent Michelle. Another successful mission. That makes, what, ten now?" The hologram was an older, brown-skinned woman with a hard, military expression.

"Citizen Hera! You're Commissioner now? Congratulations!"

Hera smiled, a forced look on a naturally grim face. "I was promoted while you were away. Thank you. I look forward to taking the Agency into a new era of influence. Before you give me your report, I want to advise that you have been issued two months of leave, on Earth or back on Vivaldis—as you prefer. You've done exceptionally well for our youngest Agent, but we don't want you to burn out."

"That's very kind of the Agency but I'm feeling great, really. Once this mission's fatigue wears off I'll be right to prep for the next."

The hologram blurred as Hera shook her head. "There is a lot of work coming up soon but other Agents can handle it. Truth to tell, Agent Michelle, there's a bit of rivalry in the ranks. *I* have faith in you, but the other five—well. I'd like to put you in reserve for a bit."

Michelle was narked. Were the other Agents jealous? How was it *her* fault if she adjusted better to the time-jumps than they?

Her vexation must have shown in her face. Hera soothed, "Just have a break, re-charge, and I'll see what I can do to have you back in the field sooner."

What could she say to that? "Thank you, Commissioner."

Michelle slept most of the space-flight back to Vivaldis, stumbled through Customs and caught a shuttle home.

"You're back!" her housemate Girion chirped, his fluro pink dreadlocks bouncing as he bowed. "How was your study trip? Did you learn lots? What are Earth men like? Would I like them?"

Stifling a yawn, Michelle slung her bag onto the floor and flopped down on a chair. "Great. Yes. Just like Vivaldan men. Probably. Do you want to get Rilaan for dinner? I have credit." She looked around the tiny apartment. Girion kept saying he'd redecorate, but when he wasn't out on dates he was studying hard for his astro-mechanics doctorate. She didn't care—she was hardly ever here. Telling him she went on study trips was the easiest explanation since her work was secret. She supposed she could afford her own apartment now that she worked for the Time-Space Agency, but frugality had been part of her nature for so long. Besides, it was nice to come home to a place that was friendly, if worn around the edges.

"Ohh! I'm meeting someone." Her friend was disappointed. Then his face lit. "Actually, you should come! His friend is into women but really shy, so we were going to help him pick up. But if you come the two of you can chat." He winked. "Nice welcome home present for you."

"I'm pretty tired…" Michelle protested. "I was looking forward to a quiet night in."

"Don't be boring!" Girion bounded into his bedroom. "Have a quick nap, take a Pep-Up and put your dancing shoes on! It'll be grand!"

Michelle grumbled but went along with it. Her social life had been severely curtailed in the last year, when she'd started running missions for the Agency.

She was annoyed at how quickly Girion went off into the club with his new boyfriend and left her with Enargo. He was an amicable looking fellow, with dark curly hair and bronze skin. Michelle envied him his colouring.

"So are you local?" she asked brightly, shrugging off her weariness.

"From Nuevos Aires," he smiled, naming a city on the other side of the planet. "And you?"

"Born right here in Vivaldis Prime."

"I'm studying at the University," he went on.

"Oh I go there!" It was a lie—she'd graduated during her traineeship at the Time-Space Agency, but the cover for the secretive nature of her job was that she was doing post-graduate study in Earth history. "What do you study?"

"History," Enargo said. "And you?"

"History as well! What a coincidence." She leaned forward and tapped the corner of her mouth. They would actually have something to talk about!

"Oh really?" He raised dark eyebrows. "What field? I haven't seen you in any of my classes."

Michelle caught the android barman's eye and signalled for service. An energising juice was in order—she didn't want to embarrass herself by yawning. "Earth History—everything from ancient right up to the intra-stellar age."

"Hmph." He didn't seem impressed. Not that she expected him to fall over with amazement but surely it was worth showing a little enthusiasm? How many people on a blind date got to meet someone who shared their field of interest? "That's really broad."

"I'm looking at long-terms patterns in human society." The lie was polished, delivered smoothly.

"Oh. Well, I'm looking at specialising in twentieth century Asian history. Asia is a geographical and cultural region of Earth that still supports the majority of the human population there. It was critical in pioneering colonist programs for our species to get off the planet."

"Yes, I know," Michelle grinned enthusiastically. "The twentieth century was a challenging time for many Asian countries. Lots of wars and new ideologies." She hoped he'd pick up that she'd said 'countries' not 'provinces' and twig that she well versed in the subject.

"Of course Asia wasn't one homogenous province, like it is now." Enargo leaned forward and Michelle shifted back. "It was divided into much smaller political divisions called 'countries'. The largest and most influential one was called China. We know Beijing to be the capital city of Earth, but back then it was only the capital city of China."

"I know," Michelle replied, a little confused. Even primary school kids knew that fact. Was he lecturing her? She'd hoped for an intellectual conversation. *It's not a competition on who knows the most.* Despite that thought, she couldn't help herself. "The rise of Japan as a military power and the subsequent clash with the rest of Asia and then the United States and allies is an interesting topic in that era."

She was being a smart-arse. One of her recent missions had involved the winding up of what was known as World War Two. She had failed to prevent the Nagasaki bombing, which had upset her badly, but one of her colleagues had managed to correct the timeline working through Soviet side. The history that was now overwritten existed only in special computers in the Time-Space Agency on Vivaldis and Earth. Michelle had spent half her recovery time going over the new history of those weeks.

"Japan was a collection of densely populated islands to the east of China. During the twentieth century they rose as a military power and invaded many other countries in Asia. They also declared war on the United States of America by bombing Pearl Harbour. Pearl Harbour was a naval base of the United States in a series of islands called Hawaii, in the Pacific Ocean…" He kept going.

Michelle was astounded. Had he swallowed an encyclopaedia program? He'd completely ignored what she'd said, instead seizing on the topic to prove his expertise. All keenness she'd felt for the evening evaporated. She stared across the dancefloor and sipped her juice as Enargo droned on.

Michelle was dying to tell him to shut up, he was boring the hell out of her, but her work training had rubbed off. She observed him and the people in the club. It was getting busy.

The music got louder. Enargo compensated by raising his voice.

I know! I was there! She screamed internally as he talked about how journalists and photographers changed history by bringing war into the living rooms of the Western World during the Vietnam conflict.

"Will you excuse me?" She stood abruptly. Enargo frowned, peering up at her. "I've just seen a friend of mine. I'll be right back." She wended her way through the crowd and skirted the dance floor, ducking between a laughing pair of blue-furred Mayash.

"Girion!" She yelled in her housemate's ear. "This date is a dud, I'm going home!"

"Bit of a stud? Don't stress, Shelly babe! I won't be home till tomorrow—apartment's all yours!" He winked and turned back to his boyfriend, who kissed him passionately.

Michelle growled then turned to spot Enargo honing in on her. *Crap, he's coming over.* She looked frantically for an escape. She launched herself over the bar and slid down past the juice dispensers. Several androids beeped warnings at her as she scooted past and burst out the door into the cool night air of the alley beyond.

The music from the club muffled now, she heaved a sigh of relief.

First thing tomorrow I'm send a com to Commissioner Hera requesting early termination of my leave. She stepped out and headed towards the nearest monorail station. *I'd rather go back to work than go on another date!*

STRENGTH TO STRENGTH

The best part about having two female protagonists is I get to write two strong, but very different, women. I can explore what it means to be a strong woman in different settings, without stereotyping what it means to be strong.

Case in point: my main character, Gwyn, is nineteen when we first meet her—bit of a dreamer, has a romantic streak. Yet when she is placed under extremely difficult circumstances—namely, is flung back in time to a violent siege—she not only survives; she escapes, forges friendships and ultimately saves some of the people she cares about. Yet she hasn't lost her romantic side—she is confronted by uncomfortable realties and emotions, doesn't always behave in a way she might be proud of, is frustrated and often frightened, yet still struggles on in an effort to do what is right.

Michelle on the other hand, fulfils the trope of bad-ass action hero; kicking butts and taking names. Adaptable, ruthless and determined, she perseveres through intense physical discomfort in order to do her duty. She is extremely capable and confident, so she fears little, knowing she will be able to fight her way out of trouble.

These two characters clash. It's easy to call Michelle the strong one, but when you consider how Gwyn not only survives, but succeeds, without any of the physical and psychological training Michelle has, you realise how, despite her flaws, Gwyn has a strength of character that continues to grow despite the hardships thrown at it. Michelle's personality risks hardening to breaking point, however, once her support systems are taken away, and it's only through some painful self-reflection that she admits that Gwyn's coping mechanisms are simply different, not weaker.

Right now I am part way through the last book in this five book time-travel series. I've had the opportunity to showcase each of my protagonists' strengths and weaknesses—alone and together—and while they have formed a working partnership, their respect for each other doesn't mean they are now best friends. Strong women don't have to be the same. They don't have to even be friends and have the same interests.

I am surrounded by strong women in my life, some of them very different. Capable, resourceful, powerful women—they achieve in many different areas of life. They are all managers to one degree or another: whether in actual job name, project managing multi-million dollar projects, or organising finances, renovations, teaching a classroom full of excitable and challenging students. Many of them are mothers—they have the strength to get up for the sixth time that night to a crying baby, corral toddlers out the door with lunches, nappies, spare clothes, water bottles. The strength of mind to deal with a relentless, unpredictable landscape. Many of them are creatives or academics, with the self-discipline to see through a multi-year project, persevering in the face of thankless tasks, with only themselves to hate or blame when the self-doubt overwhelms them in the seemingly endless days.

But they carry on. They survive, they improve, they thrive—particularly in the company of other strong women. And it is that theme I have sought to draw out in my books, that alone, a strong woman is strong, but together—with others—she is incredible.

OTHER SHORT STORIES

NAUGHTY ZOMBIES

The night was dark, and the wind whipped through the trees. The park gate creaked on its hinges. In the playground the swings swayed back and forth with a quiet, eerie screech. A late night jogger paused at gate, considering doing a quick lap of the park, but the dark shadows of the trees seemed to be moving and something about the place made it seem not quite deserted. The jogger pressed on, suddenly eager to be home and behind closed doors.

By day the park was quaint and pleasant, populated with tall old trees and worn wooden benches. The metal playground consisted of a creaking swing-set and rust-spotted slide that had not yet been replaced by council for newer, plastic equipment, whose bright colours would have looked out of place against the dry grass. Not that any of that would have been evident on this dark night, with no moon and grey clouds scudding across the sky. A spooky atmosphere filled the park, and things that would have been normal by day seemed frightening and weird.

Just then the wind dropped and a strange muttering could be heard. It would have chilled the bones of anyone fool enough to be out on a night like this.

"Brains... Brains..."

Something sounded like it was lurching closer. The sound of shuffling feet and morbid groaning echoed through the night.

"Brains... Brains!"

Suddenly a slightly petulant voice interrupted. *Cough.* "Why does it always have to be brains?"

"<u>Brai</u>-- what?"

The petulance decreased slightly and tried to take on a reasonable tone. "I said: why does it always have to be brains? I mean, there are plenty of other parts to a person. Legs and arms and other bits and pieces. Saying 'brains' is a bit boring after awhile."

The shuffling and groaning stopped and an embarrassed silence grew.

"I'm just saying," came the defensive mutter.

An exasperated huff came in reply. "We're zombies. 'Brains' is what we say!"

Another voice interjected. "She's got a point, Greg. I know I get a bit tired of saying 'brains' all the time."

Greg spluttered with indignation. "What is this, a bloody committee? We've always said 'brains'--that's how people know we're zombies. If we didn't say 'brains' they'd just think we were drunks and tell us to piss off!" Someone tried to respond but he rode over the top of them. "And how can you be tired, you're undead!"

<u>Cough</u>. "Figure of speech, Greg."

"Anyway, no one is going to mistake us for drunks," the first protestor added. "Not once we start ripping limbs off. It's not even like we eat just brains. We'll sink our teeth into anything."

"Yeah, Greg," another voice chimed in. "And if they do think we're drunks it just lets us get closer to them. People watch a lot of zombie shows these days. They twig pretty early, then leg it."

A murmur of agreement went through the group. "It sure is hard to catch anyone when all you can do is shuffle."

"Mmm."

"Yeah."

Yet another voice chimed in. "Why can't we move a bit faster, anyway? Plenty of movies have zombies that run and even jump these days. And I'm not just talking about the classic 'jump-scare' that Doreen here has perfected."

Respectful nods ensued, albeit slightly carefully in the case of those whose heads were only attached with sinews of grey, rotting skin. Everyone knew zombies were famous for jump-scares, but it was a lot harder than it looked. Even the lurching took a lot of practice, to get the forward-yet-sideways motion just so. Many zombies had put their hips out dragging their legs at awkward angles.

"Yes, well, I'm sure Doreen is to be congratulated for practising so hard, but the point is, we shuffle, and we say 'brains!' because that's what zombies do! It's traditional!" Greg sounded a bit narky. Everyone remembered he had been known to run morning classes on the correct intonation of 'brains', so it probably wasn't surprising he was taking this personally.

"Don't get worked up, Greg," one voice said soothingly.

"I'm not getting worked up!" he snapped. "I just don't see why this has suddenly turned into a bloody round-table discussion of appropriate zombie behaviour!"

This time the awkward silence was broken by Doreen's voice piping up, "We just want to try something different, Greg. That's all." She trailed off uncertainly.

"We? Who's we?" he demanded. "Come on, you lot have been talking about this behind my back, haven't you?"

Shuffle, shuffle.

"Fine. Just fine! Do what you like then! Forget tradition and correct zombie—"

"Greg, I really do think you are overreacting just a little," the soother's voice said. "We just want to have a little fun."

"Fun? What do you mean, fun? The hell with fun!"

Several minutes later one of the others finally spoke. "Would have had a bit more impact if he'd stormed off. The shuffle just doesn't have the same effect when you're trying to make a dramatic exit."

Several heads shook sadly. "Poor old Greg, he really is committed to tradition."

"Bugger tradition," the voice that had complained about the slowness of shuffling continued. "Haven't you seen World War Z? Those bastards can <u>move</u>. The old shuffling zombie that groans and mutters 'brains' is on its way out. We've got to get with the times."

Everyone murmured in agreement.

"Does that mean we can say what we like now?" Doreen wanted to know.

"Well, I am," the voice that had sparked the whole debate sounded defiant. "If I want to say 'legs' or 'ears' I will!"

"Arms..."

"Feet..."

"Elbows..."

They considered this. "Maybe not 'elbows'," someone said. "Sounds a bit odd."

"What about 'bum'?" someone else wanted to know. A nervous titter was heard.

"Heehee. Or 'boobs'?" chimed in another. Chuckles spread through the group. Others started coming up with suggestions of their own.

"Willy!"

"Tits!"

"Fanny!"

The cries got more raucous as the zombies poured out of the park, sprinting down the road and leaping onto cars. By morning the infestation had spread through the city, and zombies would never be the same again.

ZOMBIE REVOLUTION

"Welcome to the Fifty-Fifth Annual Zombie Festival of Culture! To begin our proceedings, we are very honoured to have as guest speaker, Ms Doreen Liu!"

Raucous applause greeted the famed leader of the revolution, one of the few that remained upright and conversant. Most of the others had long succumbed to war wounds and deterioration, their bodies literally falling apart.

"Thank you, thank you." Doreen took to the stage. She was the picture of zombie respectability: pearls delicately hiding the stitches in her neck, an elegant pantsuit tailored to fit her diminutive form. "It is a privilege to be here today, fifty-five years after the revolution which marked our ascent as the dominant death-form here on this planet."

More cheers. Several zombie girls in the audience snapped their Z-phones and twittered to each other with excitement. "She's my absolute hero!" one said. "Ever since I did that project on her at school."

Up on stage, Doreen paused and smiled graciously, a picture of yellow chipped teeth and stretched grey skin. "To begin this festival, it is my great pleasure to announce the first event: the Zombie Spelling Bee!"

The judges took their place, Doreen seated beside them, and the contestants filed in. Zombie children, bursting with nerves and pride to be a part of this competition, and in front of such a distinguished audience. The first contestant stood to the fore, his hands twitching.

"Zachary Pinsman, please spell for us 'cardiovascular'," a sonorous judge intoned.

"Cardiovascular.   C-a-r-d-i-o-v-a-s…c-u-l-a-r. Cardiovascular."

The audience applauded. A small scuffle took place up the back when one zombie man clapped too hard and knocked his own hand off. "Found it!" he shouted and craning necks returned to look at the stage. Doreen tsked quietly. "Some zombies just don't know how to behave," a judge murmured to her.

The spelling bee continued. Neurological, Achilles and rhomboids were just some of the words set for the participants.

"A decidedly anatomical theme to this year," one zombie lady whispered to her husband.

Competitors were eliminated when they failed to spell a word correctly. It came down to two, the first lad, Zachary, and a quietly-spoken young zombie girl called Kate.

"The winner shall be decided by a single word," the deep-voiced female judge told them. "I shall read the word, and the first competitor to finish spelling it correctly shall be proclaimed the winner. Are you ready, Zachary and Kate?"

The zombie children nodded vigorously. They weren't yet at the stage of having to worry about sinews detaching spontaneously and appendages falling off.

"The word is…" the judge opened an envelope and unfolded the paper inside it. She read the word and raised her eyebrows, but opened her mouth all the same. "The word to spell is… *brains.*"

Gasps ricocheted around the hall. "Disgusting!" one voice cried. "I didn't bring my children here to listen to profanities," a male zombie declared.

"Silence!" the judge bellowed.

Everyone looked at the stage. Doreen was perched on her stool, rigid with shock. The other judges didn't know where to look. Zachary Pinsman had frozen. It was one thing to *know* a swear word—it was another thing to say it out loud in front of your mum and all these adult zombies!

A small piping voice broke through the air. "Brains. B-r-a-i-n-s. Brains." It was little Kate Mossman.

"We have a winner!" the head judge declared.

* * *

The rest of the festival was somewhat marred by that first event, though of course no one liked to say so. Several families left that day, forgoing their weekend pass, and an official statement was put out to visitors that a full investigation into the organisation of the Zombie Spelling Bee would take place without delay.

"I will not tolerate it!" Doreen slammed a delicate grey palm down on the table. "How did this even happen? I thought a full vetting process took place for the Cultural Festival, to make sure all content is appropriate."

Other zombies shifted uncomfortably. Only the head judge from the Spelling Bee remained placid. "Times change, Ms Liu. There are a number of zombies who feel that 'brains' is no longer an offensive word." She ignored the flinches from around the room.

"Ms Mendoza," Doreen leaned forward and spoke dangerously to the judge. "I didn't risk my limbs creating a new future for all zombie-kind just to have it *mocked* by a *child!* Consider yourself off the Festival Committee." She flounced out, the effect ruined somewhat by her knocking her hand on the doorframe and one of her fingers flying off. Doreen stalked back into the room, retrieved the offending digit and glared at them all before exiting again.

Silence.

"She can't actually fire me, you know," Ms Mendoza remarked. "It's not a job. I just volunteer two weeks of the year to help get things organised." But no one would meet her gaze.

"Right." She frowned at her knuckles, wishing she could crack them. Knowing her luck they'd just smoosh. "I'll just let myself out then."

* * *

It took time, but Carla Mendoza was annoyed enough at her humiliation to start talking to other zombies. Quietly at first (no one wanted to upset the establishment) but with persistence. Soon feelings of repression bubbled out and within months there were protests in the streets and petitions to the government. The backlash followed from zombies who felt Mendoza's movement was a betrayal of everything the Revolution stood for, but the protestors would not be stopped.

"This is ridiculous!" the zombie Minister for Education declared at the next cabinet meeting. "Prime Minister, this is all a fad that will blow over in another few weeks. We have more important things to worry about than rabble rousers in the street."

"I fear not." The Prime Minister turned her head carefully, wary of breaking skin. "They've pulled up a figure from history and made a martyr of him. Saint Greg, they called him, though the Reaper only knows we've left that kind of illogical religiosity behind us."

"But then what should we do?" the Minister for Trade asked in a quavering voice. "Are there concessions we can make?"

"Concessions!" The Prime Minister was furious. "I will not concede to these hooligans! We will crush them if need be."

"What's that noise?" another minister said suddenly. They all paused. A dull droning teased the edges of their hearing.

"It sounds like…" one started to say.

"Nothing! It sounds like nothing!" The Prime Minister walked to the window to shut the blind, but then gasped.

"Brains! *Brains!*" They could all hear it now. The cabinet ministers rushed to the window and goggled at the sight of hundreds, no thousands, of protestors. The mass of zombies lurched towards Government House. They were slow, but they were inexorable. Security guards were overwhelmed. Vicious snarls floated up to higher levels where zombie politicians and civil workers screamed in panic. It wasn't over quickly. The Prime Minister and her cabinet bolted themselves into her office but the sheer weight of zombie protestors against the door was too much. The hinges simply squealed their surrender and the door crashed inwards. It was carnage.

Quite some hours later, Carla Mendoza held a press-conference in the gore spattered Elliptical Office. "This is a great day for all zombie-kind!" she declared, her grey skin showing small tears and nicks from fighting. Z-phones snapped photos and excited journalists jotted notes. "Today is the day we took back freedom! Today is the day we returned to our zombie heritage, and thus built a future for ourselves!"

Cheers resounded. Mendoza smiled. "My first act as Prime Minister," she announced, "will be to introduce the mandatory teaching of the word 'brains' into our school curriculum. Correct lurching deportment will also be taught, and jump-scares will become part of physical education…"

THE JOB

It was the hardest job she'd ever done. The hours were ridiculous; shiftwork like you wouldn't believe! And the breaks—what breaks? Surely there were laws about that? But it wasn't as if she was on any kind of award wage. Conditions that would have any Fair Work official objecting were completely ignored in this industry. Sure, there was no uniform and she didn't have to travel far, but the negative aspects far outweighed the positive ones in this instance.

And her boss. Well, he was the real reason this job was so hard. Poor communicator? Tick. Extremely emotional? Tick. Yells, screams, changes his mind? Tick! Tick! Tick!

But there was no point saying it wasn't fair. "If you didn't want this job, why did you quit your old one?" people would ask. Ooh, her old boss would surely love to see her come crawling back, to say she couldn't hack it. Well, she wouldn't give them the satisfaction! She'd take the abuse and the shitty hours and just suck it up. Push through it. Surely once she got the hang of things it would get easier? As long as she didn't kill herself or her boss in the meantime...

"How's things?" people wanted to know.

"Oh, you know." She'd smile brightly and drown her voice in false cheer. "Getting there!"

She couldn't ask for help. Too much pride. Too much pressure. Had to be seen to be succeeding. Keep on top of things. Otherwise people would think she was a failure. She'd *know* she was a failure.

Keep smiling, keep performing. "Oh, you are doing a good job!" they would say. "It's hard, but obviously you are managing well!" They didn't see the tears. The frustration. They didn't know how she dreaded waking up each morning, unable to face another endless day at work. She'd crawl into bed and dream of it, or worse, lie awake thinking of it, knowing she needed her rest but unable to do so, then hating herself even more for it.

The hate. That was it. She hated herself for taking this job. She hated her boss. But she couldn't say that. Oh no. That wasn't allowed. Instead it ate up inside of her, poisoning the times when her boss was in a good mood, or not hassling her. She was on edge all the time, waiting for the next crisis, the next demand. She couldn't enjoy her time off, even when she got away from work. It was all she could think about and she felt guilty that she wasn't better at her job.

Finally it got too much. Something snapped. Her boss was screaming at her so she simply turned around and walked out of the room. Outside, into the fresh air. She felt like she hadn't seen the sun in an age.

Phone out. Dial.

"Mum?"

"Hi, honey! How are you?"

Silence.

"Honey? Are you there? Is everything okay?"

"Mum." Voice cracking. She could still hear her boss screaming inside. He was really furious this time.

"Honey, what's wrong?"

"Mum, I need help. I'm not coping. I'm scared..."

It was a lifesaving phone call. She didn't quit her job, oh no. But once she'd been diagnosed with post-natal depression the air, while still not clear, was breathable. She didn't have to be okay. There was help, for her and her baby.

THE VOICE

'Oh, Connor sleeps through, he's so clever.' The mum's voice is smug, at least in my ears. I don't hear the replies of the other mums in the group, but I know what they are thinking.

Look at that new mum. Look how tired she is. Her baby was crying when she came in. I bet she doesn't know what she's doing.

And they are right. I bite my lip in an effort not to cry. Stacey hates the car. She was screaming her head off when we arrived at the clinic.

Coming to this mums' group was a bad idea. I should have just stayed home and tried to get her to sleep.

But Stacey refuses to sleep in the cot. I do everything right; swaddle her, put her at the bottom of the cot on her back, shush her gently and rock the cot and she just screams and screams until I can't take it anymore. I always end up picking her up and rocking her to sleep. Now after eight weeks the slightest cry puts my teeth on edge. Even when she finally sleeps I dread the moment she wakes.

I hate it. Everyone said how wonderful it would be. Hard but wonderful. But I hate it.

Stacey is due for a feed soon but she's fallen asleep my arms and there's no way I'm going to wake her. If I'm lucky I'll get her into the car and be able to race home, buying myself a few precious minutes of quiet.

Why do all these other mums look like they have it so together? I'm dying inside.

'Now make sure take to advantage of the services here at the clinic,' the child health nurse says. 'You can weigh bub, talk to our breastfeeding nurses, touch base about post-natal depression warning signs.'

I cringe at those words. *I can't be depressed. I'm smarter than that. I just have to keep going and tough it out. I don't need help. Don't want everyone to think I'm a failure.*

The session ends. I rush out the door, cradling Stacey. My oversized nappy bag crashes into the doorframe. Reaching the car I turn the ignition, winding the windows down and blasting the air-con in an effort to cool the car.

'Hey, you've got a real cutie there.' One of the other mums—I can't remember her name—is parked next to me. Her little boy sleeps with his face smooshed on her shoulder, dark curly hair askew.

Shit. What's her name? God, I'm so hopeless. 'Thanks.' I try to smile. 'Your boy is gorgeous too.'

'Hey, do you have anywhere to be right now?' the woman asks. 'I don't really want to go home just yet, so wondered if you maybe wanted to grab a coffee? There's a shop just around the corner. If I put Lee in the car he's bound to wake up.'

Coffee? No, I should just go home. Can't afford coffee—we're on one income now. 'Um.'

'Please?' The woman smiles. 'I could really use the company, and you seemed nice in the group.'

Nice? I barely said a word. Didn't dare. I would have started crying. Barely holding it together now. 'I shouldn't,' I whisper.

'Coffee *and* cake?'

I give a half-hearted laugh. 'Oh, I better not. Trying to lose the baby weight and that.'

'Fuck that,' the woman says. 'Are you breast-feeding?' I nod. 'Then you need cake. You burn five hundred calories a day, and I don't know about you but when I'm up sixteen times a night I need frickin coffee.'

'Um, okay.' I'm being weak. I should go home. Put Stacey in the cot. I have to train her to sleep or I'll go insane. But I turn off the car and follow the woman—*what's her name? God, I'm hopeless!*

'I'm really sorry,' the woman says when we reach the coffee shop. 'I've forgotten your name. Brain like a sieve these days.'

The smell of roasted beans and warm milk soothes me and I giggle. I tell her my name. "And this is Stacey. And, um, I've forgotten yours.'

'Kelly and Lee.' Kelly smiles and settles Lee onto her other shoulder.

'I thought it was just me,' I chuckle but then begin to cry. Great, fat tears roll down my cheeks and my body shakes. Stacey grizzles and I try to shush her but the sobs just turned into hiccups and my daughter scrunches up her face and wails.

'Hey! Hey!' Kelly reaches over and pats my shoulder. 'It's okay, hon.'

'I'm so sorry!' I wipe my nose with the back of my hand, repositioning Stacey in an effort to rock her back to sleep. *You loser! Oh, how fucking hopeless are you? Crying in front of a complete stranger, in the middle of a coffee shop.* Customers raise their heads like a field of cattle and stare. 'I should go.'

'Hey, no.' Kelly puts out her hand. 'Hey, can we sit up the back in a booth?' she asks the waitress. I allow myself to be led past all the grannies munching on scones and hipsters with their turmeric lattes. The hubbub of chatter drills into my mind, critical comments and judgemental glances. I sniff and nod when Kelly orders us both a flat white. 'Lactose free. And a slice of that carrot cake—two spoons. Thanks.'

It's feeding time. I pull up my shirt and balance a nipple shield on one breast, struggling to guide Stacey's screaming mouth onto it without knocking it loose. Kelly notices.

'Oh, you're using shields? That's hard. You poor thing, tell me what's going on.'

'It's nothing. I'm sorry. I'm just a bit tired.' *So hopeless. Can't even keep it together at a coffee shop. Useless.*

'Uh, duh you're a bit tired! Bet you haven't had a full night's sleep in months! I was a hippo at the end of my pregnancy—back ached and got up every half hour to pee! Sucks! Sleep deprivation is a killer, my friend. It messes with you big time.'

'I know,' I sniff. Stacey finally latches on and sucks with the fierce determination of a starving infant. 'I guess today was just a bit harder than normal. I try not to go out much.'

'Oh, honey.' Kelly reaches out, taking my hand this time. 'Does it make you anxious to go out? I was like that with my first kid. Barely left the house. Felt sick just thinking about it. Thought everyone was judging me and saying how hopeless I was. It was awful.'

I gaze at her through bloodshot, teary eyes. 'Really?' *It's not just me?* It's as though a fist around my heart unclenches ever so slightly.

Kelly laughs. 'I was a fucking mess. Ended up in sleep school, anti-depressants, seeing a shrink. Have to say though, the help I got was the best thing ever. I was in a bad way.'

Yes, but you're probably not... a bad mother like I am. 'How... how old is your first kid?'

'Savannah? Six. Couldn't handle the thought of another baby before then. Was so terrified I'd go off the deep end again. Still on the happy pills and still seeing a counsellor from time to time. It's good maintenance.'

How does she seem so together? How come I'm falling apart?

Our coffees arrive, along with the carrot cake. 'Dig in,' Kelly orders. 'You look like you need a treat.'

That starts the tears again. Stacey falls off and I bring her upright for a burp, hauling my shirt down. I curse at the milk that leaks through my bra. 'Shit, I forgot breast pads.'

'Don't stress, hon. No one is looking, and you've got a new baby so fuck anyone who dares to judge. Half the women have been there and we're on your side.'

Stacey burps and snuffles into my neck. I love the closeness but wish desperately I could just put my daughter down. 'I just feel so hopeless all the time. I knew it would be hard, but it's killing me. I'm scared I—' I stop. *Shit, what are you doing? You almost blurted out that you're a bad mother! Shut up!*

Kelly looks at me, compassion in her eyes. 'You're scared?' she prompts gently.

Tears well up again. 'I'm scared I'm going to hurt her,' I whisper. 'I get so tired.'

Kelly nods. 'You're scared you're going to hurt her by accident? Or on purpose?'

She knows! She's going to report you or something! You aren't fit to be a mother! Yet still the words creep out. 'On purpose…' I look at Kelly, expecting damnation. 'I'm such a bad mother.'

'Oh, my dear. You poor thing. You poor, poor thing. You're not a bad mother. The fact that you're scared of that means you're a good mother.'

I stare at her, confused. Kelly nods sadly. 'I was the same. I was so out of my mind with tiredness and anxiety I was terrified I would drop Savannah, or slap her, or deliberately knock her head against the doorway. I thought I was evil. But it wasn't me thinking that, not really.'

'Huh?' I bob Stacey up and down. She rewards me with another burp.

'It's an ego-dystonic thought. That's what my shrink told me. It's the manifestation of your worst fears. You see, a bad mother, or a bad parent, wouldn't care if they hurt their child. You want to protect them, even from yourself. That means you care about them.'

'Um, I suppose?'

Kelly sighs. 'Look hon, I know we've only just met but my heart is breaking for you because you are exactly where I was five years ago. Will you please come back to the child health clinic and talk to one of the midwives there. I'll stay with you if you like? Or I can piss off if you want privacy. But please, please, please don't just go home and stew on this. Your mind is working against you right now.'

'Oh, no, I should just go home!' Even as I say it, I feel sick at the thought. The empty house. The sink full of dishes and dirty washing staring accusingly. The crying baby. My loneliness.

'That's the anxiety talking.' Kelly stabs the carrot cake and eats some, waving the fork. 'It's fucking evil. I know I seem like I'm being the biggest busy-body but I would be the shittest person if I walked away right now. Please.'

I stare at her. Maybe she's right. Maybe I do need help 'Okay…' I rearrange Stacey to keep feeding and lean awkwardly to the side to drink my luke-warm coffee.

'Good girl,' Kelly says. 'Now eat some carrot cake. It's going to be okay.'

THE PRIZE

I'm here. On the ground. Where the action is.

I'm scanning, scanning, scanning—there. Target identified.

I'm on the move, keeping low. Be careful. Wait.

Is it? Looking…

It is! It's what I'm after, go, go, go!

No!

She snatches it just before I get there! She's always there first. No matter how quick or stealthy I am she is always faster, stronger, more agile. She has it now, the prize, she taunts me with it. She knows I can't fight it off her, knows I'm not good enough.

Not yet. One day maybe. But today she waits, just out of reach, watching and daring me to have a go.

I could. Maybe… One daring move and who knows? Maybe this time I'll wrestle it free, maybe this time she'll fumble and drop it and I'll get it and I'll win.

She knows what I'm thinking. The world shrinks to just her and me. Eyes locked.

Go on, she seems to say. *I dare you to try.*

The temptation is too great, I lunge and she dashes away. Yelling, I hurtle after her, heedless of the fact that every time we've met in the field she's come out on top, that she's bigger than me.

I'm intent, all I can see is the prize.

She changes direction, too fast for me to follow. I whirl, awkward and confused. Where did she go?

There. She waits for me to have another go. I know it's pointless but like a wild thing I charge, my limbs flailing, almost falling over myself to get to her. To it.

She waits until I am almost upon her, then pulls back, but her taunting carries her too far this time. Intent on teasing me she slips and there! The prize comes towards me. I have it! I have—no!

She reaches out and knocks it loose, snatching it up again and skipping away with ease.

I can't. I just can't. It's too much and a howl of frustrated misery spirals out of my mouth. I sit, defeated, and cry to the heavens that once again, I've lost. Like I ever had a chance.

I thought we were friends. I thought we could get along. But every time the prize is dangled in front of us we go mad; nothing else matters. It's exhausting.

Footsteps. Still wailing my losses, I turn. It's her. The referee. The adjudicator. The one who calls the shots and sets the field. But she has another name too. The most important name of all.

Mummy.

"Oh, sweetheart." I hold my arms up and she lifts me. I can see her smile through my tears. "Did the silly dog steal the ball again? Never mind, you'll just have to learn to share."

And somehow, cradled in her embrace, I know that that's alright.

TROUBLE

Rhi trailed her fingers down the silky black fabric of her dress all the same. It clung to her body, made her feel good. Sexy.

"I'll be good," Rhi whispered to her cherry-lipped reflection. Mascara lined eyes blinked back at her and a seductive smile appeared at the corner of her mouth.

Of course you will, beautiful. You're just going to have a little fun.

Fun. There was no harm in going out for a few drinks with friends and having a dance.

As always, the first drink took the edge off her social awkwardness and she relaxed. Talking shit with her friends, they mocked each other and let the music rev them up. The bar was busy but not packed; the dance floor inhabited by a few early enthusiasts. Rhi would wait. She was pacing her drinks tonight—she knew she was a lightweight. But the temptation was there—to throw back a few shots and believe herself the hottest mover out there. She was still sober enough to laugh at the thought. "I'm doing well, tonight—not gonna burn out early!"

"Why, you outta cash?" Rhi's friend Michael looked concerned. "I'll buy you a drink."

"Nah, I'm good, thanks Mikey. Save it for some guy you want to pick up." She smiled and they began sussing out the talent in the bar. She was proud of herself. She was staying in control.

"Woo! I love this song!" Jiya leapt out of her seat and grabbed Rhi's hand. "Come on!"

They bopped and jerked to the beat, having fun. Rhi saw a stunning blonde girl in a short white number dancing near them and bit her lip. She never had the confidence to try to pick up girls. She was too scared of being rejected.

"Let's get another drink!" she yelled in Jiya's ear. A tequila shot later and Rhi was in the zone. A tall, well-built guy caught her eye. He wasn't spectacularly handsome but she steered away from those types anyway. They tended to be arrogant.

They spoke no words, just gravitated towards each other and danced. Beat by beat, they swirled towards each other. Grins and glances ignited the air between them, then the distance was too close and too intense for eye contact. He grabbed her hips and they sashayed as one, her back to his. She didn't know where her friends were, didn't care. She felt alive. She was on fire.

"Wanna get out of here?" His voice was deep and smooth, but she knew he felt it too. The excitement rose as they wound their way off the dance floor, forcing their way through the crush.

The cool night air was a blast of reality and Rhi blinked. "Come on," her dance partner said. "I'm staying not far."

She was glad of it. The cold breeze gave the mood a little frostbite, but their kisses in the lift up to the apartment warmed Rhi right up again. She buzzed with anticipation. Inside the door he pressed her up against it and kissed her hard. She ached in all the places her body touched his; her breasts tingled, her groin burned and his hands felt so good as they clasped her butt. A whimper of desire pressed its way out from between their kiss—small groans of wanting murmured back and forth with increased passion.

They wheeled across the room, a tangle of discarded clothes and hands inside underwear. Rhi was faintly aware of a click and a female's voice saying, "Sam?"

Rhi sprang back and almost stacked it on her high heels. She fell against the couch and sat amongst a rumpled pillow and sheet. "You have a girlfriend?" She was livid.

"Sam, what the fuck?" It was the blonde girl from the club. Like Daenerys Targaryen about to set fire to Slavers' Bay, blondie advanced on Sam and Rhi, fury and disgust in her face. Sam held up his hands in front of his naked, well-muscled torso and Rhi experienced resentment and humiliation that she'd been about to get all up in that and it had been snatched away.

Khaleesi hadn't finished. She stopped by the couch and said, "Were you about to have sex on my couch? Or just use my bed and not tell me?"

"Jen, I'm sorry, I just–"

"I can't believe you would be such a shitty guest!"

"Um, I'm just gonna go." Rhi retrieved her dress from the floor and shrugged it over her beet red face. All the alcohol she'd drunk made her head swim. "I'm so sorry—I didn't know. I'm really, really sorry."

Khaleesi—Jen—looked at her with what looked like a flicker of disappointment and… something else. Rhi got tangled in a strap and tugged in vain, then gave up and made for the door, dress mostly on but crooked.

"I'll buzz you out," Jen said, shooting a cold look at Sam. "You need the swipe, the automatic thing is broken."

Rhi didn't know what to say, so she kept silent as they went down in the lift. "I'm really sorry," she tried again as they hit the ground floor and approached the entrance. Her dress was still twisted so she pulled at the strap again.

"Here. Stop." Jen reached out a hand and helped Rhi neaten up. "Sam's not my boyfriend, just so you know." She was matter of fact. "He's just been staying at my place a few days coz our mothers are friends. He knows I don't like guys." In a different voice she went on, "I saw you at the club."

"I saw you! You're so pretty." Rhi gulped and apologised again, trying to process what she'd heard. "I'm sorry, I'm tipsy still; I just blurt anything."

Jen gave her that odd look again. Did it mean what Rhi thought it meant? "Um, I should order an Uber or something." She fumbled for her phone and tapped at the app.

Her breath caught as Jen put a hand out and placed it over Rhi's phone. Daenerys Targaryen never looked so unsure. "So… since you know where I live and all, did you want to meet up for a drink maybe sometime? I mean, unless you'd rather hang out with Sam." She smiled as if it was a joke but the echo of uncertainty haunted her eyes.

"I'd like that!" Rhi felt the electricity in her, so abruptly shut off, rise again. "Hanging out with you, that is."

Jen bit the bottom corner of her lip and Rhi was mesmerised. "I'll put my number in your phone then." Jen thumbed in a number then hit dial. Her own phone lit up. "You know it's legit, and now I have yours." She smiled and Rhi's stomach flipped as she returned the smile.

A sedan pulled up outside the apartment block and beeped. "Um, guess that's me," Rhi said. "Sorry about the, um…" she waved a hand upwards, indicating Sam and Jen's apartment.

Jen shrugged. "I'll boot him in the morning." She let her hand fall away and waved her purse near the sensor. Rhi pushed the glass door open and walked through. She turned back.

"It's Rhi, by the way."

Jen smiled. "I know. I asked your friends."

All the way home Rhi clasped her arms around herself, feeling sexy, feeling wanted, feeling thrilled.

Guess some things are worth a bit of trouble, sometimes.

She smiled.

Pablo smiled as guests wished him a happy birthday. The whole town was here, except the one person he wanted to see.

"Señor Pablo." The voice, deeper and more melodic than it had been in youth, made him turn.

"Luis. It's just Pablo. It's always been just Pablo to you." His heart thumped under his crucifix tattoo. They'd been fourteen, rebellious and learning about love.

"Are you happy, Pablo?" Luis asked, a can of beer in his gnarled hand. Farming had not been kind to him, but in his smile Pablo still saw the beautiful boy he loved.

"Why shouldn't I be happy? I have all this." Pablo gestured with his own beer, taking in the chattering party, the extensive family, the decorated home.

The two men stood in silence, their lack of words speaking volumes. Odd looks were cast—a poor farmer socialising with Señor Pablo.

"And you?" Pablo grunted. "Your family is well?"

"Thank you, they are. Maria's first babe died but she birthed the second well. I'm a grandfather now." Luis smiled, discoloured teeth testament to cigarettes and poor dentistry. Guilt ratcheted through Pablo again. His family afforded the best physicians, a luxury in this town.

"I'm happy for you."

"Are you?" Luis raised his crinkled eyes. "We're old men now, Pablo, we can be honest."

His words chipped the glass of Pablo's heart. A gulp of beer burned rather than soothed the torrent of bitterness in his throat. "Honest, Luis? We could never be honest." He was going to scream, or cry, or punch someone. Make a scene. Embarrass his family. His wife gazed over from her position as matriarch, presiding over the other dames of the town. She knew. She had always known, though they never spoke of it. He would shame his family. They didn't deserve that. He didn't deserve them.

"Pablo?"

He focussed on Luis. Concern etched itself into the lines of his friend's face.

"Come on, come sit down, have a cigarette."

Guided outside, he leant against the whitewashed wall. The closed door muted the party. He breathed in the cigarette Luis held to his lips. Memories flooded in with the nicotine. Stolen kisses behind his father's factory. The burn of the tattoo that was meant to mark their love forever.

"We should have run away, Luis." His voice croaked. "We should have gone when you said. I was wrong. I was a coward." Blinded by tears, he didn't see the arms that encircled him. He laid his head on Luis' shoulder and wept.

"Shh, mi querido. I forgave you for that a long time ago. Now you need to forgive yourself."

Bitterness warred with guilt and self-loathing in his heart. Soft, dry lips pressed his forehead. He blinked at Luis.

"I still love you, mi querido. And I have enough love for us both."

The glass melted. The resentment faded. Instead of his heart shattering like he'd expected at a lifetime of missed opportunity, it grew warm and began to heal.